POIROT WAS PUZZLED

as to why anyone would kill a man with seemingly no enemies or guilty secrets.

POIROT WAS PERPLEXED

by the alarming number of suspects who virtually demanded investigation—a monstrously powerful millionaire . . . a madcap actress . . . a corrupt gigolo . . . an idealistic terrorist . . . a repulsive secret agent . . . and a beautiful young heiress.

POIROT WAS PIQUED

by a master murderer who kept one corpse ahead of the great detective as Poirot vowed to get to the bottom of this case—even if it took him to the darkest depths of a hidden human hell.

AN OVERDOSE OF DEATH

(formerly titled *The Patriotic Murders*)

AGATHA CHRISTIE

A DELL BOOK

Published by
DELL PUBLISHING CO., INC.
1 Dag Hammarskjold Plaza
New York, N.Y. 10017

This book was originally published under
the title of THE PATRIOTIC MURDERS
by Dodd, Mead & Company, Inc.
Dell ® TM 681510, Dell Publishing Co., Inc.

ISBN: 0-440-16780-9

Reprinted by arrangement with
Dodd, Mead & Company, Inc.
Printed in the United States of America

Three Previous Dell Editions

New Dell Edition
First printing—April 1982

One, two, buckle my shoe,
Three, four, shut the door,
Five, six, pick up sticks,
Seven, eight, lay them straight,
Nine, ten, a good fat hen,
Eleven, twelve, men must delve,
Thirteen, fourteen, Maids are courting,
Fifteen, sixteen, Maids in the kitchen,
Seventeen, eighteen, Maids in waiting,
Nineteen, twenty, my plate's empty . . . .

Chapter One

ONE, TWO, BUCKLE MY SHOE

MR. MORLEY was not in the best of tempers at breakfast. He complained of the bacon, wondered why the coffee had to have the appearance of liquid mud, and remarked that breakfast cereals were each one worse than the last.

Mr. Morley was a small man with a decided jaw and a pugnacious chin. His sister, who kept house for him, was a large woman rather like a female grenadier. She eyed her brother thoughtfully and asked whether the bath water had been cold again.

Rather grudgingly, Mr. Morley said it had not.

He glanced at the paper and remarked that the government seemed to be passing from a state of incompetence to one of positive imbecility!

Miss Morley said in a deep bass voice that it was disgraceful!

As a mere woman she had always found whatever government happened to be in power distinctly useful. She urged her brother on to explain exactly *why* the government's present policy was inconclusive, idiotic, imbecile, and frankly suicidal!

When Mr. Morley had expressed himself fully on these points, he had a second cup of the despised coffee and unburdened himself of his true grievance.

"These girls," he said, "are all the same! Unreliable, self-centered—not to be depended on in any way."

Miss Morley said interrogatively, "Gladys?"

"I've just had the message. Her aunt's had a stroke and she's had to go down to Somerset."

Miss Morley said, "Very trying, dear, but after all, hardly the girl's *fault*."

Mr. Morley shook his head gloomily.

"How do I know the aunt *has* had a stroke? How do I know the whole thing hasn't been arranged between the girl and that very unsuitable young fellow she goes about with? That young man is a wrong 'un if I ever saw one! They've probably planned some outing together for to-day."

"Oh, no, dear, I don't think Gladys would do a thing like that. You know you've always found her very conscientious."

"Yes, yes."

"An intelligent girl and really keen on her work, you said."

"Yes, yes, Georgina, but that was before this undesirable young man came along. She's been quite different lately—*quite* different—absent-minded—upset—nervy."

The grenadier produced a deep sigh. She said, "After all, Henry, girls do fall in love. It can't be helped."

Mr. Morley snapped, "She oughtn't to let it affect her efficiency as my secretary. And today, in particular, I'm extremely busy! Several *very* important patients. It is *most* trying!"

"I'm sure it must be extremely vexing, Henry. How is the new boy shaping, by the way?"

Henry Morley said gloomily, "He's the worst I've had yet! Can't get a single name right and has the most uncouth manners. If he doesn't improve I shall sack him and try again. I don't know what's the good of our education nowadays. It seems to turn out a collection of nitwits who can't understand a single thing you say to them, let alone remember it."

He glanced at his watch.

"I must be getting along. A full morning, and that Sainsbury Seale woman to fit in somewhere as she is in pain. I suggested that she should see Reilly, but she wouldn't hear of it."

"Of course not," said Georgina loyally.

"Reilly's very able—very able indeed. First-class diplomas. Thoroughly up-to-date in his work."

"His hand shakes," said Miss Morley. "In my opinion he *drinks*."

Her brother laughed, his good temper restored. He said, "I'll be up for a sandwich at half past one as usual."

At the Savoy Hotel Mr. Amberiotis was picking his teeth and grinning to himself.

Everything was going very nicely.

He had had his usual luck. Fancy those few kind words of his to that idiotic hen of a woman being so richly repaid. Oh, well—*cast your bread upon the waters.* He had always been a kindhearted man. *And* generous! In the future he would be able to be even more generous. Benevolent visions floated before his eyes. Little Dimitri— And the good Constantopopolous struggling with his little restaurant— What pleasant surprises for them—

The toothpick probed unguardedly and Mr. Amberiotis winced. Rosy visions of the future faded and gave way to apprehensions of the immediate present. He explored tenderly with his tongue. He took out his notebook. *Twelve o'clock. 58 Queen Charlotte Street.*

He tried to recapture his former exultant mood, but in vain. The horizon had shrunk to six bare words: *58 Queen Charlotte Street. Twelve o'clock.*

At the Glengowrie Court Hotel, South Kensington, breakfast was over. In the lounge, Miss Sainsbury Seale was sitting talking to Mrs. Bolitho. They occupied adjacent tables in the dining-room and had made friends the day after Miss Sainsbury Seale's arrival a week ago.

Miss Sainsbury Seale said, "You know, dear, it really *has* stopped aching! Not a twinge! I think perhaps I'll ring up—"

Mrs. Bolitho interrupted her.

"Now don't be foolish, my dear. You go to the dentist and *get it over*."

Mrs. Bolitho was a tall, commanding female with a deep voice. Miss Sainsbury Seale was a woman of forty-odd with indecisively bleached hair rolled up in untidy curls. Her clothes were shapeless and rather artistic, and her pince-nez were always dropping off. She was a great talker.

She said now wistfully, "But, really, you know, it doesn't ache *at all*."

"Nonsense. You told me you hardly slept a wink last night."

"No, I didn't—no, indeed—but perhaps *now* the nerve has actually *died*."

"All the more reason to go to the dentist," said Mrs. Bolitho firmly. "We all like to put it off, but that's just cowardice. Better make up one's mind and *get it over!*"

Something hovered on Miss Sainsbury Seale's lips. Was it the rebellious murmur of, "Yes, but it's not *your* tooth!"

All she actually said, however, was, "I expect you are right. And Mr. Morley is such a careful man and really never hurts one *at all*."

The meeting of the board of directors was over. It had passed off smoothly. The report was good. There should have been no discordant note. Yet, to the sensitive Mr. Samuel Rotherstein there had been *something*, some nuance in the chairman's manner.

There had been, once or twice, a shortness, an acerbity in his tone—quite uncalled for by the proceedings.

Some secret worry, perhaps? But, somehow, Rotherstein could not connect a secret worry with Alistair Blunt. He was such an unemotional man. He was so very normal. So essentially British.

There was, of course, always liver— Mr. Rotherstein's liver gave him a bit of trouble from time to time. But he'd

never known Alistair complain of his liver. Alistair's
health was as sound as his brain and his grasp of finance.
It was not annoying heartiness—just quiet well-being.

And yet—there was *something*—once or twice the chairman's hand had wandered to his face. He had sat support-
ing his chin. Not his normal attitude. And once or twice
he had seemed actually—yes, *distrait*.

They came out of the board room and passed down the
stairs.

Rotherstein said, "Can't give you a lift, I suppose?"

Alistair Blunt smiled and shook his head.

"My car's waiting." He glanced at his watch. "I'm not
going back to the city." He paused. "As a matter of fact,
I've got an appointment with the dentist."

The mystery was solved.

Hercule Poirot descended from his taxi, paid the man,
and rang the bell of 58 Queen Charlotte Street.

After a little delay it was opened by a lad in page boy's
uniform, with a freckled face, red hair, and an earnest
manner.

Hercule Poirot said, "Mr. Morley?"

There was in his heart a ridiculous hope that Mr. Morley might have been called away, might be indisposed,
might not be seeing patients today— All in vain. The page
boy drew back, Hercule Poirot stepped inside, and the
door closed behind him with the quiet remorselessness of
unalterable doom.

The boy said, "Name, please?"

Poirot gave it to him, a door on the right of the hall was
thrown open, and he stepped into the waiting-room.

It was a room furnished in quiet good taste and, to
Hercule Poirot, indescribably gloomy. On the polished
(reproduction) Sheraton table were carefully arranged
papers and periodicals. The (reproduction) Hepplewhite
sideboard held two Sheffield plated candlesticks and an

epergne. The mantelpiece held a bronze clock and two bronze vases. The windows were shrouded by curtains of blue velvet. The chairs were upholstered in a Jacobean design of red birds and flowers.

In one of them sat a military-looking gentleman with a fierce mustache and a yellow complexion. He looked at Poirot with an air of one considering some noxious insect. It was not so much his gun he looked as though he wished he had with him, as his Flit spray. Poirot, eyeing him with distaste, said to himself, *In verity, there are some Englishmen who are altogether so unpleasing and ridiculous that they should have been put out of their misery at birth.*

The military gentleman, after a prolonged glare, snatched up the *Times,* turned his chair so as to avoid seeing Poirot, and settled down to read it.

Poirot picked up *Punch.*

He went through it meticulously, but failed to find any of the jokes funny.

The page boy came in and said, "Colonel Arrowbumby?" and the military gentleman was led away.

Poirot was speculating on the probabilities of there really being such a name, when the door opened to admit a young man of about thirty.

As the young man stood by the table, restlessly flicking over the covers of magazines, Poirot looked at him sideways. An unpleasant and dangerous looking young man, he thought, and not impossibly a murderer. At any rate he looked far more like a murderer than many of the murderers Hercule Poirot had arrested in the course of his career.

The page boy opened the door and said to mid-air, "Mr. Peerer?"

Rightly construing this as a summons to himself, Poirot rose. The boy led him to the back of the hall and round the corner to a small elevator in which he took him up to the second floor. Here he led him along a passage, opened a door which led into a little anteroom, tapped at a second door, and without waiting for a reply, opened it, and stood back for Poirot to enter.

Poirot entered to a sound of running water and came round the back of the door to discover Mr. Morley washing his hands with professional gusto at a basin on the wall.

There are certain humiliating moments in the lives of the greatest of men. It has been said that no man is a hero to his valet. To that may be added that few men are heroes to themselves at the moment of visiting their dentist.

Hercule Poirot was morbidly conscious of this fact.

He was a man who was accustomed to have a good opinion of himself. He was Hercule Poirot, superior in most ways to other men. But in this moment he was unable to feel superior in any way whatever. His morale was down to zero. He was just that ordinary, that craven figure, a man afraid of the dentist's chair.

Mr. Morley had finished his professional ablutions. He was speaking now in his encouraging professional manner.

Hardly as warm as it should be, was it, for the time of year?

Gently he led the way to the appointed spot—to The Chair! Deftly he played with its headrest, running it up and down.

Hercule Poirot took a deep breath, stepped up, sat down, and relaxed his head to Mr. Morley's professional fiddlings.

"There," said Mr. Morley with hideous cheerfulness. "That quite comfortable? Sure?"

In sepulchral tones Poirot said that it was quite comfortable.

Mr. Morley swung his little table nearer, picked up his little mirror, seized an instrument, and prepared to get on with the job.

Hercule Poirot grasped the arms of the chair, shut his eyes, and opened his mouth.

"Any special trouble?" Mr. Morley inquired.

Slightly indistinctly, owing to the difficulty of forming consonants while keeping the mouth open, Hercule Poirot was understood to say that there was no special trouble. This was indeed the twice yearly overhaul that his sense of order and neatness demanded. It was, of course, possible that there might be nothing to do— Mr. Morley might, perhaps, overlook that second tooth from the back from which those twinges had come— He *might*—but it was unlikely—for Mr. Morley was a very good dentist.

Mr. Morley passed slowly from tooth to tooth, tapping and probing, murmuring little comments as he did so.

"That filling is wearing down a little—nothing serious, though. Gums are in pretty good condition, I'm glad to see." A pause at a suspect, a twist of the probe—no, on again; false alarm. He passed to the lower side. One, two— on to three? No— *The dog,* Hercule Poirot thought in confused idiom, *has seen the rabbit!*

"A little trouble here. Not been giving you any pain? H'm, I'm surprised." The probe went on.

Finally Mr. Morley drew back, satisfied.

"Nothing very serious. Just a couple of fillings—and a trace of decay on that upper molar. We can get it all done, I think, this morning."

He turned on a switch and there was a hum. Mr. Morley unhooked the drill and fitted a needle to it with loving care.

"Guide me," he said briefly, and started the dread work.

It was not necessary for Poirot to avail himself of this permission, to raise a hand, to wince, or even to yell. At exactly the right moment, Mr. Morley stopped the drill, gave the brief command, "Rinse," applied a little dressing, selected a new needle, and continued. The ordeal of the drill was terror rather than pain.

Presently, while Mr. Morley was preparing the filling, conversation was resumed.

"Have to do this myself this morning," he explained. "Miss Nevill has been called away. You remember Miss Nevill?"

Poirot untruthfully assented.

"Called away to the country by the illness of a relative. Sort of thing that *does* happen on a busy day. I'm behind-hand already this morning. The patient before you was late. Very vexing when that happens. It throws the whole morning out. Then I have to fit in an extra patient because she is in pain. I always allow quarter of an hour in a morning in case that happens. Still, it adds to the rush."

Mr. Morley peered into his little mortar as he ground. Then he resumed his discourse.

"I'll tell you something that I've always noticed, M. Poirot. The big people—the important people—they're always on time—never keep you waiting. Royalty, for instance. Most punctilious. And these big city men are the same. Now this morning I've got a most important man coming—Alistair Blunt!"

Mr. Morley spoke the name in a voice of triumph.

Poirot, prohibited from speech by several rolls of cotton wool and a glass tube that gurgled under his tongue, made an indeterminate noise.

Alistair Blunt! Those were the names that thrilled nowadays. Not dukes, not earls, not prime ministers. No, plain Mr. Alistair Blunt. A man whose face was almost unknown to the general public—a man who only figured in an occasional quiet paragraph. Not a spectacular person.

Just a quiet nondescript Englishman who was the head of the greatest banking firm in England. A man of vast wealth. A man who said yes and no to governments. A man who lived a quiet, unobtrusive life and never appeared on a public platform or made speeches. Yet a man in whose hands lay supreme power.

Mr. Morley's voice still held a reverent tone as he stood over Poirot ramming the filling home.

"Always comes to his appointments absolutely on time. Often sends his car away and walks back to his office. Nice, quiet, unassuming fellow. Fond of golf and keen on his garden. You'd never dream he could buy up half Europe! Just like you and me."

A momentary resentment rose in Poirot at this offhand coupling of names. Mr. Morley was a good dentist, yes, but there *were* other good dentists in London. There was only *one* Hercule Poirot.

"Rinse, please," said Mr. Morley.

"It's the answer, you know, to their Hitlers and Mussolinis and all the rest of them," went on Mr. Morley, as he proceeded to tooth number two. "We don't make a fuss over here. Look how democratic our King and Queen are. Of course, a Frenchman like you, accustomed to the Republican idea—"

"I ah nah a Frahah—I ah—ha a Benyon."

"Tchut—tchut—" said Mr. Morley sadly. "We must have the cavity completely dry." He puffed hot air relentlessly on it.

Then he went on. "I didn't realize you were a Belgian. Very interesting. Very fine man, King Leopold, so I've always heard. I'm a great believer in the tradition of royalty myself. The training is good, you know. Look at the remarkable way they remember names and faces. All the result of training—though, of course, some people have a natural aptitude for that sort of thing. I, myself, for instance. I don't remember names, but it's remarkable the way I never forget a face. One of my patients the other day, for instance—I've seen that patient before. The name meant nothing to me—but I said to myself at once, 'Now where have I met you before?' I've not remembered yet— but it will come back to me—I'm sure of it. Just another rinse, please."

The rinse accomplished, Mr. Morley peered critically into his patient's mouth.

"Well, I think that seems all right. Just close—very gently— Quite comfortable? You don't feel the filling at all? Open again, please. No, that seems quite all right."

The table swung back, the chair swung round.

Hercule Poirot descended, a free man.

"Well, good-by, M. Poirot. Not detected any criminals in my house, I hope?"

Poirot said with a smile, "Before I came up, everyone looked to me like a criminal! Now, perhaps, it will be different!"

"Ah, yes, a great deal of difference between before and after! All the same, we dentists aren't such devils now as we used to be! Shall I ring for the elevator for you?"

"No, no, I will walk down."

"As you like—the elevator is just by the stairs."

Poirot went out. He heard the faucets start to run as he closed the door behind him.

He walked down the two flights of stairs. As he came to the last bend, he saw the Anglo-Indian colonel being shown out. Not at all a bad-looking man, Poirot reflected mellowly. Probably a fine shot who had killed many a tiger. A useful man—a regular outpost of empire.

He went into the waiting-room to fetch his hat and stick which he had left there. The restless young man was still there somewhat to Poirot's surprise. Another patient, a man, was reading the *Field*.

Poirot studied the young man in his newborn spirit of kindliness. He still looked very fierce—and as though he wanted to do a murder—but not really a murderer— thought Poirot kindly. Doubtless, presently, this young man would come tripping down the stairs, his ordeal over, happy and smiling and wishing no ill to anyone.

The page boy entered and said firmly and distinctly, "Mr. Blunt."

The man at the table laid down the *Field* and got up. A man of middle height, of middle age, neither fat nor thin. Well dressed, quiet.

He went out after the boy.

One of the richest and most powerful men in England— but he still had to go to the dentist just like anybody else, and no doubt felt just the same as anybody else about it!

These reflections passing through his mind, Hercule Poirot picked up his hat and stick and went to the door. He glanced back as he did so, and the startled thought went through his mind that that young man must have a very bad toothache indeed.

In the hall Poirot paused before the mirror there to adjust his mustaches, slightly disarranged as the result of Mr. Morley's ministrations.

He had just completed their arrangement to his satisfaction when the elevator came down again and the page boy emerged from the back of the hall whistling discordantly. He broke off abruptly at the sight of Poirot and came to open the front door for him.

A taxi had just drawn up before the house and a foot was protruding from it. Poirot surveyed the foot with gallant interest.

A neat ankle, quite a good quality stocking. Not a bad foot. But he didn't like the shoe. A brand new patent-leather shoe with a large gleaming buckle. He shook his head.

Not chic—very provincial!

The lady got out of the taxi, but in doing so she caught her other foot in the door and the buckle was wrenched off. It fell tinkling to the pavement. Gallantly Poirot sprang forward and picked it up, restoring it with a bow.

Alas! Nearer fifty than forty. Pince-nez. Untidy yellow-gray hair—unbecoming clothes—those depressing art greens! She thanked him, again dropping her pince-nez, then her handbag.

Poirot, polite if no longer gallant, picked them up for her.

She went up the steps of 58 Queen Charlotte Street, and Poirot interrupted the taxi driver's disgusted contemplation of a meager tip.

"You are free, *hein?*"

The taxi driver said gloomily, "Oh, I'm *free.*"

"So am I," said Hercule Poirot. "Free of care!"

He saw the taxi man's air of deep suspicion.

"No, my friend, I am not drunk. It is that I have been to the dentist and I need not go again for six months. It is a beautiful thought."

Chapter Two

THREE, FOUR, SHUT THE DOOR

IT WAS A QUARTER TO THREE when the telephone rang. Hercule Poirot was sitting in an easy chair, happily digesting an excellent lunch. He did not move when the bell rang but waited for the faithful George to come and take the call.

"*Eh bien,*" he said, as George, with a "Just a minute, sir," lowered the receiver.

"It's Chief Inspector Japp, sir."

"Aha!"

Poirot lifted the receiver to his ear.

"*Eh bien, mon vieux,*" he said. "How goes it?"

"That you, Poirot?"

"Naturally."

"I hear you went to the dentist this morning? Is that so?"

Poirot murmured, "Scotland Yard knows everything!"

"Man by the name of Morley. Fifty-eight Queen Charlotte Street."

"Yes." Poirot's voice had changed. "Why?"

"It was a genuine visit, was it? I mean you didn't go to stir him up or anything of that sort?"

"Certainly not. I had three teeth filled if you want to know."

"What did he seem like to you—manner much as usual?"

"I should say so, yes. Why?"

Japp's voice was rigidly unemotional.

"Because not so very much later he shot himself."

"What?"

Japp said sharply, "That surprises you?"

"Frankly, it does."

Japp said, "I'm not too happy about it myself. I'd like to have a talk with you. I suppose you wouldn't like to come round?"

"Where are you?"

"Queen Charlotte Street."

Poirot said, "I will join you immediately."

It was a police constable who opened the door of Number 58. He said respectfully, "M. Poirot?"

"It's I, myself."

"The Chief Inspector is upstairs. Second floor—you know it?"

Hercule Poirot said, "I was there this morning."

There were three men in the room. Japp looked up as Poirot entered.

He said, "Glad to see you, Poirot. We're just going to move him. Like to see him first?"

A man with a camera who had been kneeling near the body got up.

Poirot came forward. The body was lying near the fireplace.

In death Mr. Morley looked very much as he had looked in life. There was a little blackened hole just below his right temple. A small pistol lay on the floor near his outflung right hand.

Poirot shook his head gently.

Japp said, "All right, you can move him now."

They took Mr. Morley away. Japp and Poirot were left alone.

Japp said, "We're through all the routine. Fingerprints, and so forth."

Poirot sat down. He said, "Tell me."

Japp pursed up his lips. He said, "He *could* have shot himself. He probably *did* shoot himself. There are only his fingerprints on the gun—but I'm not quite satisfied."

"What are your objections?"

"Well, to begin with, there doesn't seem to be any reason *why* he should shoot himself— He was in good health, he was making money, he hadn't any worries that anyone knew of. He wasn't mixed up with a woman—at least," Japp corrected himself cautiously, "as far as we know, he wasn't. He hasn't been moody or depressed or unlike himself. That's partly why I was anxious to hear what *you* said. You saw him this morning, and I wondered if you'd noticed anything."

Poirot shook his head.

"Nothing at all. He was—what shall I say?—normality itself."

"Then that makes it odd, doesn't it? Anyway, you wouldn't think a man would shoot himself in the middle of business hours, so to speak. Why not wait till this evening? That would be the natural thing to do."

Poirot agreed.

"When did the tragedy occur?"

"Can't say exactly. Nobody seems to have heard the shot. But I don't think they would. There are two doors between here and the passage and they have baize fitted round the edges—to deaden the noise from the victims of the dental chair, I imagine."

"Very probably. Patients under gas sometimes make a lot of noise."

"Quite. And outside, in the street, there's plenty of traffic, so you wouldn't be likely to hear it out there."

"When was it discovered?"

"Round about one-thirty—by the page boy, Alfred Biggs. Not a very bright specimen, by all accounts. It seems that Morley's twelve-thirty patient kicked up a bit of a row at being kept waiting. About one-ten the boy came up and knocked. There was no answer and apparently he didn't dare come in. He'd got in a few rows already from Morley and he was nervous of doing the wrong thing. He went down again and the patient walked out in a huff at one-fifteen. I don't blame her. She'd been kept waiting three-quarters of an hour and she wanted her lunch."

"Who was she?"

Japp grinned.

"According to the boy she was Miss Shirty—but from the appointment book her name was Kirby."

"What system was there for showing up patients?"

"When Morley was ready for his next patient he pressed that buzzer over there and the boy then showed the patient up."

"And Morley pressed the buzzer last?"

"At five minutes past twelve, and the boy showed up the patient who was waiting. Mr. Amberiotis, Savoy Hotel, according to the appointment book."

A faint smile came to Poirot's lips. He murmured, "I wonder what our page boy made of *that* name!"

"A pretty hash, I should say. We'll ask him presently if we feel like a laugh."

Poirot said, "And at what time did this Mr. Amberiotis leave?"

"The boy didn't show him out, so he doesn't know. A good many patients just go down the stairs without ringing for the elevator and let themselves out."

Poirot nodded.

Japp went on, "But I rang up the Savoy Hotel. Mr. Amberiotis was quite precise. He said he looked at his watch as he closed the front door and it was then twenty-five minutes past twelve."

"He could tell you nothing of importance?"

"No, all he could say was that the dentist had seemed perfectly normal and calm in his manner."

"*Eh bien,*" said Poirot. "Then that seems quite clear. Between five and twenty past twelve and half past one something happened—and presumably nearer the former time."

"Quite. Because otherwise—"

"Otherwise he would have pressed the buzzer for the next patient."

"Exactly. The medical evidence agrees with that for what it's worth. The divisional surgeon examined the body—at twenty past two. He wouldn't commit himself—they never do nowadays—too many individual idiosyncrasies, they say. But Morley couldn't have been shot *later* than one o'clock, he says—probably considerably earlier—but he wouldn't be definite."

Poirot said thoughtfully, "Then at twenty-five minutes past twelve our dentist is a normal dentist, cheerful, urbane, competent. And after that? Despair—misery—what you will—and he shoots himself."

"It's funny," said Japp. "You've got to admit, it's funny."

"Funny," said Poirot, "is not the word."

"I know it isn't really—but it's the sort of thing one says. It's odd, then, if you like that better."

"Was it his own pistol?"

"No, it wasn't. He hadn't got a pistol. Never had had one. According to his sister there wasn't such a thing in the house. There isn't in most houses. Of course, he *might* have bought it if he'd made up his mind to do away with himself. If so, we'll soon know about it."

Poirot asked, "Is there anything else that worries you?"

Japp rubbed his nose.

"Well, there was the way he was lying. I wouldn't say a man *couldn't* fall like that—but it wasn't quite *right* somehow! And there was just a trace or two on the carpet—as though something had been dragged along it."

"That, then, is decidedly suggestive."

"Yes, unless it was that dratted boy. I've a feeling that *he* may have tried to move Morley when he found him. He denies it, of course, but then he was scared. He's that kind of young ass. The kind that's always putting his foot in it and getting cursed, and so they come to lie about things almost automatically."

Poirot looked thoughtfully round the room. At the wash basin on the wall behind the door, at the tall filing-cabinet on the other side of the door. At the dental chair and surrounding apparatus near the window, then along to the fireplace and back to where the body had lain; there was a second door in the wall near the fireplace.

Japp had followed his glance.

"Just a small office through there." He flung open the door.

It was as he had said, a small room, with a desk, a table with a spirit lamp and tea apparatus, and some chairs. There was no other door.

"This is where his secretary worked," explained Japp. "Miss Nevill. It seems she's away today."

His eyes met Poirot's.

The latter said, "He told me, I remember. That again—might be a point against suicide?"

"You mean she was *got* out of the way?"

Japp paused. He said, "If it *wasn't* suicide, he was murdered. But why? That solution seems almost as unlikely as the other. He seems to have been a quiet, inoffensive sort of chap. Who would want to murder him?"

Poirot said, "Who *could* have murdered him?"

Japp said, "The answer to that is—almost anybody! His sister could have come from their flat above and shot him, one of the servants could have come in and shot him. His partner, Reilly, could have shot him. The boy Alfred could have shot him. One of the patients could have shot him." He paused and said, "*And Amberiotis could have shot him*—easiest of the lot."

Poirot nodded.

"But in that case—we have to find out why?"

"Exactly. You've come round again to the original problem. Why? Amberiotis is staying at the Savoy. Why does a rich Greek want to come and shoot an inoffensive dentist?

That's really going to be our stumbling-block. *Motive!"*

Poirot shrugged his shoulders. He said, "It would seem that death selected, most inartistically, the wrong man. The Mysterious Greek, the Rich Banker, the Famous Detective—how natural that one of *them* should be shot! For mysterious foreigners may be mixed up in espionage and rich bankers have connections who will benefit by their deaths and famous detectives may be dangerous to criminals."

"Whereas, poor old Morley wasn't dangerous to anybody," observed Japp gloomily.

"I wonder."

Japp whirled round on him.

"What's up your sleeve now?"

"Nothing. A chance remark."

He repeated to Japp those few casual words of Mr. Morley's about recognizing faces, and his mention of a patient.

Japp looked doubtful.

"It's possible, I suppose. But it's a bit farfetched. It must have been someone who wanted his identity kept dark. You didn't notice any of the other patients this morning?"

Poirot murmured, "I noticed in the waiting-room a young man who looked exactly like a murderer!"

Japp said, startled, "What's that?"

Poirot smiled. *"Mon cher,* it was upon my arrival here! I was nervous, fanciful—*enfin,* in a *mood.* Everything seemed sinister to me, the waiting-room, the patients, the very carpet on the stairs! Actually, I think the young man had a very bad toothache. That was all!"

"I know what it can be," said Japp. "However, we'll check up on your murderer all the same. We'll check up on *everybody,* whether it's suicide or not. I think the first thing is to have another talk with Miss Morley. I've only had a word or two. It was a shock to her, of course, but she's the kind that doesn't break down. We'll go and see her now."

Tall and grim, Georgina Morley listened to what the two men had to say and answered their questions. She said with emphasis, "It's incredible to me—*quite* incredible—that my brother should have committed suicide!"

Poirot said, "You realize the alternative, mademoiselle?"

"You mean—murder." She paused. Then she said slowly, "It is true—that alternative seems nearly as impossible as the other."

"But not *quite* as impossible?"

"No—because—oh, in the first case, you see, I am speaking of *something I know*—that is, my brother's state of mind. I *know* he had nothing on his mind—I *know* that there was no reason—no reason *at all* why he should take his own life!"

"You saw him this morning—before he started work?"

"At breakfast—yes."

"And he was quite as usual—not upset in any way?"

"He was upset—but not in the way you mean. He was just annoyed!"

"Why was that?"

"He had a busy morning in front of him, and his secretary and assistant had been called away."

"That is Miss Nevill?"

"Yes."

"What did she do for him?"

"She did all his correspondence, of course, and kept the appointment book, and filed all the charts. She also saw to the sterilizing of the instruments and ground up his fillings and handed them to him when he was working."

"Had she been with him long?"

"Three years. She is a very reliable girl and we are—were both very fond of her."

Poirot said, "She was called away owing to the illness of a relative, so your brother told me."

"Yes, she got a telegram to say her aunt had had a stroke. She went off to Somerset by an early train."

"And that was what annoyed your brother so much?"

"Ye-es." There was a faint hesitation in Miss Morley's answer. She went on rather hurriedly. "You—you mustn't think my brother unfeeling. It was only that he thought—just for a moment—"

"Yes, Miss Morley?"

"Well, that she might have played truant on purpose. Oh, please don't misunderstand me—I'm quite certain that Gladys would *never* do such a thing. I told Henry so. But the fact of the matter is, that she has got herself engaged to rather an unsuitable young man—Henry was very vexed about it—and it occurred to him that this young man *might* have persuaded her to take a day off."

"Was that likely?"

"No, I'm sure it wasn't. Gladys is a very conscientious girl."

"But it is the sort of thing the young man might have suggested?"

Miss Morley sniffed.

"Quite likely, I should say."

"What does he do, this young fellow—what is his name, by the way?"

"Carter, Frank Carter. He is—or was—an insurance clerk, I believe. He lost his job some weeks ago and doesn't seem able to get another. Henry said—and I daresay he was right—that he is a complete rotter. Gladys had actually lent him some of her savings and Henry was very annoyed about it."

Japp said sharply, "Did your brother try to persuade her to break her engagement?"

"Yes, he did, I know."

"Then this Frank Carter would, quite possibly, have a grudge against your brother."

The grenadier said robustly, "Nonsense—that is if you are suggesting that Frank Carter shot Henry. Henry advised the girl against young Carter, certainly; but she didn't take his advice—she is foolishly devoted to Frank."

"Is there anyone else you can think of who had a grudge against your brother?"

Miss Morley shook her head.

"Did he get on well with his partner, Mr. Reilly?"

Miss Morley replied acidly, "As well as you can ever hope to get on with an Irishman!"

"What do you mean by that, Miss Morley?"

"Well, Irishmen have hot tempers and they thoroughly enjoy a row of any kind. Mr. Reilly liked arguing about politics."

"That was all?"

"That was all. Mr. Reilly is unsatisfactory in many ways, but he was very skilled in his profession—or so my brother said."

Japp persisted. "How is he unsatisfactory?"

Miss Morley hesitated, then said acidly, "He drinks too much—but please don't let that go any further."

"Was there any trouble between him and your brother on that subject?"

"Henry gave him one or two hints. In dentistry," continued Miss Morley didactically, "a steady hand is needed, and an alcoholic breath does *not* inspire confidence."

Japp bowed his head in agreement. Then he said, "Can you tell us anything of your brother's financial position?"

"Henry was making a good income and he had a certain amount put by. We each had a small private income of our own left to us by our father."

Japp murmured with a slight cough, "You don't know, I suppose, if your brother left a will?"

"He did—and I can tell you its contents. He left a hundred pounds to Gladys Nevill, otherwise everything comes to me."

"I see. Now—"

There was a fierce thump on the door. Alfred's face then appeared round it. His goggling eyes took in each detail of the two visitors as he ejaculated, "It's Miss Nevill. She's back—and in a bad state. Shall she come in, she wants to know?"

Japp nodded and Miss Morley said, "Tell her to come here, Alfred."

"Okay," said Alfred, and disappeared.

Miss Morley said with a sigh and in obvious capital letters, "That Boy is a Sad Trial."

Gladys Nevill was a tall, fair, somewhat anemic girl of about twenty-eight. Though obviously very upset, she at once showed that she was capable and intelligent.

Under the pretext of looking through Mr. Morley's papers, Japp got her away from Miss Morley down to the little office next door to the surgery.

She repeated more than once, "I simply *cannot* believe it! It seems quite incredible that Mr. Morley should do such a thing!"

She was emphatic that he had not seemed troubled or worried in any way.

Then Japp began, "You were called away today, Miss Nevill—"

She interrupted him. "Yes, and the whole thing was a wicked practical joke! I do think it's awful of people to do things like that. I really do."

"What do you mean, Miss Nevill?"

"Why, there wasn't anything the matter with Aunt at all. She'd never been better. She couldn't understand it when I suddenly turned up. Of course, I was ever so glad— but it did make me mad. Sending a telegram like that and upsetting me and everything."

"Have you got that telegram, Miss Nevill?"

"I threw it away, I think, at the station. It just said 'Your aunt had stroke last night. Please come at once.'"

"You are quite sure—well—" Japp coughed delicately "—that it wasn't your friend, Mr. Carter, who sent that telegram?"

"Frank? Whatever for? Oh! I see, you mean—a put-up job between us? No, indeed, Inspector—neither of us would do such a thing."

Her indignation seemed genuine enough and Japp had a little trouble in soothing her down. But a question as to the patients on this particular morning restored her to her competent self.

"They are all here in the book. I daresay you have seen it already. I know about most of them. Ten o'clock Mrs. Soames—that was about her new plate. Ten-thirty Lady Grant—she's an elderly lady—lives in Lowndes Square. Eleven o'clock M. Hercule Poirot, he comes regularly—oh, of course, this *is* him—sorry, M. Poirot, but I really am *so* upset! At eleven-thirty, Mr. Alistair Blunt—that's the banker, you know—a short appointment, because Mr. Morley had prepared the filling last time. Then Miss Sainsbury Seale—she rang up specially—had toothache and so Mr. Morley fitted her in. A terrible talker she is, never stops—the fussy kind, too. Then at twelve o'clock Mr. Amberiotis —he was a new patient—made an appointment from the Savoy Hotel. Mr. Morley gets quite a lot of foreigners and Americans. Then twelve-thirty Miss Kirby. She comes up from Worthing."

Poirot asked, "There was here when I arrived a tall military gentleman. Who would he be?"

"One of Mr. Reilly's patients, I expect. I'll just get his list for you, shall I?"

"Thank you, Miss Nevill."

She was absent only a few minutes. She returned with a book similar to that of Mr. Morley's.

She read out, "Ten o'clock Betty Heath (That's a little girl of nine.) ; eleven o'clock, Colonel Abercrombie."

"Abercrombie!" murmured Poirot. *"C' était ça!"*

"Eleven-thirty, Mr. Howard Raikes. Twelve o'clock, Mr. Barnes, and that was all the patients this morning. Mr.

Reilly isn't so booked up as Mr. Morley, of course."

"Can you tell us anything about any of these patients of Mr. Reilly's?"

"Colonel Abercrombie has been a patient for a long time, and all of Mrs. Heath's children come to Mr. Reilly. I can't tell you anything about Mr. Raikes or Mr. Barnes, though I fancy I have heard their names. I take all the telephone calls, you see—"

Japp said, "We can ask Mr. Reilly ourselves. I should like to see him as soon as possible."

Miss Nevill went out. Japp said to Poirot, "All old patients of Mr. Morley's *except Amberiotis*. I'm going to have an interesting talk with Mr. Amberiotis presently. He's the last person, as it stands, to see Morley alive, and we've got to make quite sure that when he last saw him, Morley *was* alive."

Poirot said slowly, shaking his head, "You have still to prove motive."

"I know. That's what is going to be the teaser. But we may have something about Amberiotis at the Yard." He added sharply, "You're very thoughtful, Poirot!"

"I was wondering about something."

"What was it?"

Poirot said with a faint smile, "Why Chief Inspector Japp?"

"Eh?"

"I said, 'Why Chief Inspector Japp?' An officer of your eminence—is he usually called in to a case of suicide?"

"As a matter of fact, I happened to be near by at the time. At Lavenham's—in Wigmore Street. Rather an ingenious system of frauds they've had there. They telephoned me there to come on here."

"But *why* did they telephone you?"

"Oh, that—that's simple enough. Alistair Blunt. As soon as the Divisional Inspector heard *he'd* been here this morning, he got on to the Yard. Mr. Blunt is the kind of person we take care of in this country."

"You mean that there are people who would like him—out of the way?"

"You bet there are. The Reds, to begin with. It's Blunt and his group who are standing solid behind the present government. Good sound conservative finance. That's why, if there were the least chance that there was any funny stuff intended against him this morning, they wanted a thorough investigation."

Poirot nodded.

"That is what I more or less guessed. And that is the feeling I have"—he waved his hands expressively—"that there was, perhaps—a *hitch* of some kind. The proper victim was—should have been—Alistair Blunt. Or is this only a beginning—the beginning of a campaign of some kind? I smell—I smell—" he sniffed the air "—big money in this business!"

Japp said, "You're assuming a lot, you know."

"I am suggesting that *ce pauvre Morley* was only a pawn in the game. Perhaps he knew something—perhaps he told Blunt something—or they feared he *would* tell Blunt something—"

He stopped as Gladys Nevill re-entered the room.

"Mr. Reilly is busy on an extraction case," she said. "He will be free in about ten minutes if that will be all right?"

Japp said that it would. In the meantime, he said, he would have another talk with the boy Alfred.

Alfred was divided between nervousness, enjoyment, and a morbid fear of being blamed for everything that had occurred! He had only been a fortnight in Mr. Morley's employ, and during that fortnight he had consistently and unvaryingly done everything wrong. Persistent blame had sapped his self-confidence.

"He was a bit rattier than usual, perhaps," said Alfred in answer to a question, "but nothing else as I remember.

I'd never have thought he was going to do himself in."

Poirot interposed.

"You must tell us," he said, "everything that you can remember about this morning. You are a very important witness, and your recollections may be of immense service to us."

Alfred's face was suffused by vivid crimson and his chest swelled. He had already given Japp a brief account of the morning's happenings. He proposed now to spread himself. A comforting sense of importance oozed into him.

"I can tell you orl right," he said. "Just you ask me."

"To begin with, did anything out of the way happen this morning?"

Alfred reflected a minute and then said rather sadly, "Can't say as it did. It was orl just as usual."

"Did any strangers come to the house?"

"No, sir."

"Not even among the patients?"

"I didn't know as you meant the patients. Nobody come what hadn't got an appointment, if that's what you mean. They were all down in the book."

Japp nodded.

Poirot asked, "Could anybody have walked in from outside?"

"No, they couldn't. They'd have to have a key, see?"

"But it was quite easy to leave the house?"

"Oh, yes, just turn the handle and go out and pull the door to after you. As I was saying, most of 'em do. They often come down the stairs while I'm taking up the next party in the elevator, see?"

"I see. Now just tell us who came first this morning and so on. Describe them if you can't remember the names."

Alfred reflected a minute. Then he said, "Lady with a little girl, that was for Mr. Reilly, and a Mrs. Soap or some such name for Mr. Morley."

Poirot said, "Quite right. Go on."

"Then another elderly lady—bit of a swell she was—come in a Daimler. As she went out a tall military gent come in, and just after him, *you* came." He nodded to Poirot.

"Right."

"Then the American gent came—"

Japp said sharply, "American?"

"Yes, sir. Young fellow. He was American all right—you could tell by his voice. Come early, he did. His appointment wasn't till eleven-thirty—and what's more he didn't keep it—neither."

Japp said sharply, "What's that?"

"Not him. Come in for him when Mr. Reilly's buzzer went at eleven-thirty—a bit later it was, as a matter of fact, might have been twenty to twelve—and he wasn't there. Must have funked it and gone away." He added with a knowing air, "They do sometimes."

Poirot said, "Then he must have gone out soon after me?"

"That's right, sir. You went out after I'd taken up a swell what come in a Rolls. Oh—it was a lovely car—Mr. Blunt's. Then I come down and let you out and a lady in. Miss Some Berry Seal, or something like that—and then I—well, as a matter of fact, I just nipped down to the kitchen to get a bite to eat, and when I was down there the buzzer went—Mr. Reilly's buzzer—so I come up and as I say, the American gentleman had gone out. I went and told Mr. Reilly and he swore a bit, as is his way."

Poirot said, "Continue."

"Lemme see, what happened next? Oh, yes, Mr. Morley's buzzer went for that Miss Seal, and the swell came down and went out as I took Miss Whatsername up in the elevator. Then I come down again and two gentlemen came—one a little man with a funny squeaky voice—I can't remember his name. For Mr. Reilly, he was. And a fat foreign gentleman for Mr. Morley.

"Miss Seal wasn't very long—not above a quarter of an

hour. I let her out and then I took up the foreign gentleman. I'd already taken the other gent in to Mr. Reilly right away as soon as he came."

Japp said, "And you didn't see Mr. Amberiotis, the foreign gentleman, leave?"

"No, sir, I can't say as I did. He must have let himself out. I didn't see either of those two gentlemen go."

"Where were you from twelve o'clock onward?"

"I always sits in the elevator, sir, waiting until the front door bell or one of the buzzers goes."

Poirot said, "And you were perhaps reading?"

Alfred blushed again.

"There ain't no harm in that, sir. It's not as though I could be doing anything else."

"Quite so. What were you reading?"

"*Death at 11:45*, sir. It's an American detective story. It's a corker, sir, it really is! All about gunmen."

Poirot smiled faintly. He said, "Would you hear the front door close from where you were?"

"You mean anyone going out? I don't think I should, sir. What I mean is I shouldn't *notice* it! You see, the elevator is right at the back of the hall and a little round the corner. The bell rings just behind it, and the buzzers, too. You can't miss *them*."

Poirot nodded and Japp asked, "What happened next?"

Alfred frowned in a supreme effort of memory.

"Only the last lady, Miss Shirty. I waited for Mr. Morley's buzzer to go, but nothing happened, and at one o'clock, the lady who was waiting, she got rather ratty."

"It did not occur to you to go up before and see if Mr. Morley was ready?"

Alfred shook his head very positively.

"Not me, sir. I wouldn't have dreamed of it. For all I knew the last gentleman was still up there. I'd got to wait for the buzzer. Of course, if I'd knowed as Mr. Morley had done himself in—"

Alfred shook his head with morbid relish.

Poirot asked, "Did the buzzer usually go before the patient came down, or the other way about?"

"Depends. Usually the patient would come down the stairs and then the buzzer would go. If they rang for the elevator, that buzzer would go perhaps as I was bringing them down. But it wasn't fixed in any way. Sometimes Mr. Morley would be a few minutes before he rang for the next patient. If he was in a hurry, he'd ring as soon as they were out of the room."

"I see—" Poirot paused and then went on. "Were you surprised at Mr. Morley's suicide, Alfred?"

"Knocked all of a heap, I was. He hadn't no call to go doing himself in as far as *I* can see—oh!" Alfred's eyes grew large and round. "Oo—er—he wasn't *murdered,* was he?"

Poirot cut in before Japp could speak.

"Supposing he was, would it surprise you less?"

"Well, I don't know, sir, I'm sure. I can't see who'd want to murder Mr. Morley. He was—well, he was a very *ordinary* gentleman, sir. Was he *really* murdered, sir?"

Poirot said gravely, "We have to take every possibility into account. That is why I told you you would be a very important witness and that you must try and recollect everything that happened this morning."

He stressed the words and Alfred frowned with a prodigious effort of memory.

"I can't think of anything else, sir. I can't indeed."

Alfred's tone was rueful.

"Very good, Alfred. And you are quite sure no one except patients came to the house this morning?"

"No *stranger* did, sir. That Miss Nevill's young man came round—and in a bad state not to find her here."

Japp said sharply, "When was that?"

"Some time after twelve it was. When I told him Miss Nevill was away for the day, he seemed very put out and he said he'd wait and see Mr. Morley. I told him Mr.

Morley was busy right up to lunchtime, but he said never mind, he'd wait."

Poirot asked, "And did he wait?"

A startled look came into Alfred's eyes. He said, "Oh— I never thought of that! He went into the waiting-room, *but he wasn't there later*. He must have got tired of waiting and thought he'd come back another time."

When Alfred had gone out of the room, Japp said sharply, "D'you think it was wise to suggest murder to that lad?"

Poirot shrugged his shoulders.

"I think so—yes. Anything suggestive that he *may* have seen or heard will come back to him under the stimulus, and he will be keenly alert to everything that goes on here."

"All the same, we don't want it to get about too soon."

"*Mon cher,* it will not. Alfred reads detective stories— Alfred is enamored of crime. Whatever Alfred lets slip will be put down to Alfred's morbid criminal imagination."

"Well, perhaps you are right, Poirot. Now we've got to hear what Reilly has to say."

Mr. Reilly's surgery and office were on the first floor. They were as spacious as the ones above but had less light in them, and were not quite so richly appointed.

Mr. Morley's partner was a tall dark young man, with a plume of hair that fell untidily over his forehead. He had an attractive voice and a very shrewd eye.

"We're hoping, Mr. Reilly," said Japp, after introducing himself, "that you can throw some light on this matter."

"You're wrong then, because I can't," replied the other. "I'd say this—that Henry Morley was the last person to go taking his own life. *I* might have done it—but *he* wouldn't."

"Why might you have done it?" asked Poirot.

"Because I've oceans of worries," replied the other. "Money troubles, for one! I've never yet been able to suit my expenditure to my income. But Morley was a careful man. You'll find no debts, nor money troubles, I'm sure of that."

"Love affairs?" suggested Japp.

"Is it Morley you mean? He had no joy of living at all! Right under his sister's thumb he was, poor man."

Japp went on to ask Reilly details about the patients he had seen that morning.

"Oh, I fancy they're all square and aboveboard. Little Betty Heath, she's a nice child—I've had the whole family one after another. Colonel Abercrombie's an old patient, too."

"What about Mr. Howard Raikes?" asked Japp.

Reilly grinned broadly.

"The one who walked out on me? He's never been to me before. I know nothing about him. He rang up and particularly asked for an appointment this morning."

"Where did he ring up from?"

"Holborn Palace Hotel. He's an American, I fancy."

"So Alfred said."

"Alfred should know," said Mr. Reilly. "He's a film fan, our Alfred."

"And your other patient?"

"Barnes? A funny precise little man. Retired civil servant. Lives out Ealing way."

Japp paused a minute and then said, "What can you tell us about Miss Nevill?"

Mr. Reilly raised his eyebrows.

"The bee-yewtiful blond secretary? Nothing doing, old boy! Her relations with old Morley were perfectly pure—I'm sure of it."

"I never suggested they weren't," said Japp, reddening slightly.

"My fault," said Reilly. "Excuse my filthy mind, won't you? I thought it might be an attempt on your part to *cherchez la femme*.

"Excuse me for speaking your language," he added parenthetically to Poirot. "Beautiful accent, haven't I? It comes of being educated by nuns."

Japp disapproved of this flippancy. He asked, "Do you know anything about the young man Miss Nevill is engaged to? His name is Carter, I understand. Frank Carter."

"Morley didn't think much of him," said Reilly. "He tried to get la Nevill to turn him down."

"That might have annoyed Carter?"

"Probably annoyed him frightfully," agreed Mr. Reilly cheerfully.

He paused and then added, "Excuse me, this *is* a suicide you are investigating, not a murder?"

Japp said sharply, "If it was a murder, would you have anything to suggest?"

"Not I! I'd like it to be Georgina! One of those grim females with temperance on the brain. But I'm afraid Georgina is full of moral rectitude. Of course, I could easily have nipped upstairs and shot the old boy myself, but I didn't. In fact, I can't imagine *anyone* wanting to kill Morley. But then I can't conceive of his killing himself."

He added—in a different voice, "As a matter of fact, I'm very sorry about it. You mustn't judge by my manner. That's just nervousness, you know. I was fond of old Morley and I shall miss him."

Japp put down the telephone receiver. His face, as he turned to Poirot, was rather grim.

He said, "Mr. Amberiotis 'isn't feeling very well—would rather not see anyone this afternoon.' He's going to see me—*and* he's not going to give me the slip, either! I've got a man at the Savoy ready to trail him if he tries to make a getaway."

Poirot said thoughtfully, "You think Amberiotis shot Morley?"

"I don't know. *But he was the last person to see Morley*

alive. And he was a new patient. According to *his* story, he left Morley alive and well at twenty-five minutes past twelve. That may be true or it may not. If Morley *was* all right, then we've got to reconstruct what happened next. *There was still five minutes to go before his next appointment.* Did someone come in and see him during that five minutes? Carter, say? Or Reilly? What happened? Depend upon it, by half past twelve, or five and twenty to one at the latest, *Morley was dead*—otherwise he'd either have sounded his buzzer or else sent down word to Miss Kirby that he couldn't see her. No, either he was killed, or else somebody told him something which upset the whole tenor of his mind, and he took his own life."

He paused.

"I'm going to have a word with every patient he saw this morning. There's just the possibility that he *may* have said something to one of them that will put us on the right track."

He glanced at his watch.

"Mr. Alistair Blunt said he could give me a few minutes at four-fifteen. We'll go to him first. His house is on Chelsea Embankment. Then we might take the Sainsbury Seale woman on our way to Amberiotis. I'd prefer to know all we can before tackling our Greek friend. After that, I'd like a word or two with the American who, according to you, 'looked like murder.' "

Hercule Poirot shook his head.

"Not murder—toothache."

"All the same, we'll see this Mr. Raikes. His conduct was queer to say the least of it. And we'll check up on Miss Nevill's telegram *and* on her aunt *and* on her young man. In fact, we'll check up on everything and everybody!"

Alistair Blunt had never loomed large in the public eye. Possibly because he was himself a very quiet and retiring man. Possibly because for many years he had functioned as a prince consort rather than as a king.

Rebecca Sanseverato, nee Arnholt, came to London a disillusioned woman of forty-five. On either side she came of the royalty of wealth. Her mother was an heiress of the European family of Rothersteins. Her father was the head of the great American banking house of Arnholt's. Rebecca Arnholt, owing to the calamitous deaths of two brothers and a cousin in an air accident, was sole heiress to immense wealth. She married a European aristocrat with a famous name, Prince Felipe di Sanseverato. Three years later she obtained a divorce and custody of the child of the marriage, having spent two years of wretchedness with a well-bred scoundrel whose conduct was notorious. A few years later her child died.

Embittered by her sufferings, Rebecca Arnholt turned her undoubted brains to the business of finance—the aptitude for it ran in her blood. She associated herself with her father in banking.

After his death she continued to be a powerful figure in the financial world with her immense holdings. She came to London—and a junior partner of the London house was sent to Claridge's to see her with various documents. Six months later the world was electrified to hear that Rebecca Sanseverato was marrying Alistair Blunt, a man nearly twenty years younger than herself.

There were the usual jeers—and smiles. Rebecca, her friends said, was really an incurable fool where men were concerned! First Sanseverato—now this young man. Of course, he was only marrying her for her money. She was in for a second disaster! But to everyone's surprise the marriage was a success. The people who prophesied that Alistair Blunt would spend her money on other women were wrong. He remained quietly devoted to his wife. Even after her death, ten years later, when as inheritor of her vast wealth he might have been supposed to cut loose, he did not marry again. He lived the same quiet and simple life. His genius for finance had been no less than his wife's. His judgments and dealings were sound—his integrity above question. He dominated the vast Arnholt and Rotherstein interests by his sheer ability.

He went very little into society, had a house in Kent and one in Norfolk where he spent week-ends—not with gay parties, but with a few quiet, stodgy friends. He was fond of golf and played moderately well. He was interested in his garden.

This was the man toward whom Chief Inspector Japp and Hercule Poirot were bouncing along in a somewhat elderly taxi.

The Gothic House was a well-known feature on Chelsea Embankment. Inside it was luxurious with an expensive simplicity. It was not very modern but it was eminently comfortable.

Alistair Blunt did not keep them waiting. He came to them almost at once.

"Chief Inspector Japp?"

Japp came forward and introduced Hercule Poirot. Blunt looked at him with interest.

"I know your name, of course, M. Poirot. And surely—somewhere—quite recently—" He paused, frowning.

Poirot said, "This morning, monsieur, in the waiting-room of *ce pauvre M. Morley.*"

Alistair Blunt's brow cleared. He said, "Of course. I knew I had seen you somewhere." He turned to Japp. "What can I do for you? I am extremely sorry to hear about poor Morley."

"You were surprised, Mr. Blunt?"

"Very surprised. Of course, I knew very little about him, but I should have thought him a most unlikely person to commit suicide."

"He seemed in good health and spirits then, this morning?"

"I think so—yes." Alistair Blunt paused, then said with

an almost boyish smile, "To tell you the truth I'm a most awful coward about going to the dentist. And I simply hate that beastly drill thing they run into you. That's why I really didn't notice anything much. Not till it was over, you know, and I got up to go. But I must say Morley seemed perfectly natural then. Cheerful and busy."

"You had been to him often?"

"I think this was my third or fourth visit. I've never had much trouble with my teeth until the last year. Breaking up, I suppose."

Hercule Poirot asked, "Who recommended Mr. Morley to you originally?"

Blunt drew his brows together in an effort of concentration.

"Let me see now—I had a twinge—somebody told me Morley of Queen Charlotte Street was the man to go to—No, I can't for the life of me remember who it was. Sorry."

Poirot said, "If it should come back to you, perhaps you will let one of us know?"

Alistair Blunt looked at him curiously.

He said, "I will—certainly. Why? Does it matter?"

"I have an idea," said Poirot, "that it might matter very much."

They were going down the steps of the house when a car drew up in front of it. It was a car of sporting build—one of those cars from which it is necessary to wriggle from under the wheel in sections.

The young woman who did so appeared to consist chiefly of arms and legs. She had finally dislodged herself as the men turned to walk down the street.

The girl stood on the pavement looking after them. Then, suddenly and vigorously, she ejaculated, "Hi!"

Not realizing that the call was addressed to them, neither man turned, and the girl repeated, "Hi! Hi! You, there!"

They stopped and looked round inquiringly. The girl walked toward them. The impression of arms and legs remained. She was tall, thin, and her face had an intelligence and aliveness that redeemed its lack of actual beauty. She was dark with a deeply tanned skin.

She said, addressing Poirot, "I know who *you* are—you're the detective man, Hercule Poirot!" Her voice was warm and deep, with a trace of American accent.

Poirot said, "At your service, mademoiselle."

Her eyes went on to his companion. Poirot said, "Chief Inspector Japp."

Her eyes widened—almost it seemed with alarm. She said—and there was a slight breathlessness in her voice, "What have you been doing here? Nothing—nothing has happened to Uncle Alistair, has it?"

Poirot said quickly, "Why should you think so, mademoiselle?"

"It hasn't? Good."

Japp took up Poirot's question.

"Why should you think anything had happened to Mr. Blunt, Miss—"

He paused inquiringly.

The girl said mechanically, "Olivera. Jane Olivera." Then she gave a slight and rather unconvincing laugh. "Sleuths on the doorstep rather suggest bombs in the attic, don't they?"

"There's nothing wrong with Mr. Blunt, I'm thankful to say, Miss Olivera."

She looked directly at Poirot.

"Did he call you in about something?"

Japp said, *"We* called on *him,* Miss Olivera, to see if he could throw any light on a case of suicide that occurred this morning."

She said sharply, "Suicide? Whose? Where?"

"A Mr. Morley, a dentist, of fifty-eight Queen Charlotte Street."

"Oh!" said Jane Olivera blankly. "Oh—" She stared ahead of her frowning. Then she said unexpectedly, "Oh, but that's absurd!" And turning on her heel she left them abruptly and without ceremony, running up the steps of the Gothic House and letting herself in with a key.

"Well!" said Japp, staring after her, "that's an extraordinary thing to say."

"Interesting," observed Poirot mildly.

Japp pulled himself together, glanced at his watch, and hailed an approaching taxi.

"We'll have time to take the Sainsbury Seale on our way to the Savoy."

Miss Sainsbury Seale was in the dimly lit lounge of the Glengowrie Court Hotel, having tea.

She was flustered by the appearance of a police officer in plain clothes—but her excitement was of a pleasurable nature, he observed. Poirot noticed, with sorrow, that she had not yet sewed the buckle on her shoe.

"Really, officer," fluted Miss Sainsbury Seale, glancing round, "I really don't know where we could go to be private. So difficult—just teatime—but perhaps you would care for some tea—and—and your friend?"

"Not for me, madam," said Japp. "This is M. Hercule Poirot."

"Really?" said Miss Sainsbury Seale. "Then perhaps— you're sure—you won't either of you have tea? No? Well, perhaps we might try the drawing-room, though that's very often full. Oh, I see there is a corner over there—in the recess. The people are just leaving. Shall we go there—"

She led the way to the comparative seclusion of a sofa and two chairs in an alcove. Poirot and Japp followed her, the former picking up a scarf and a handkerchief that Miss Sainsbury Seale had shed en route.

He restored them to her.

"Oh, thank you—so careless of me. Now please, Inspector —no, Chief Inspector, isn't it?—*do* ask me anything you like. So distressing the whole business. Poor man—I suppose he had something on his mind? Such worrying times we live in!"

"Did it seem to you he was worried, Miss Sainsbury Seale?"

"Well—" Miss Sainbury Seale reflected, and finally said unwillingly, "I can't really say, you know, that he *did!* But then perhaps I shouldn't notice—not under the *circumstances.* I'm afraid I'm rather a *coward,* you know." Miss Sainsbury Seale tittered a little and patted her bird's-nest-like curls.

"Can you tell us who else was in the waiting-room while you were there?"

"Now let me see—there was just one young man there when I went in. I think he was in pain because he was muttering to himself and looking quite wild and turning over the leaves of a magazine just anyhow. And then suddenly he jumped up and went out. Really *acute* toothache he must have had."

"You don't know whether he left the house when he went out of the room?"

"I don't know at all. I imagined he just felt he couldn't wait any longer and *must* see the dentist. But it couldn't have been Mr. Morley he was going to, because the boy came in and took me up to Mr. Morley only a few minutes later."

"Did you go into the waiting-room again on your way out?"

"No. Because you see, I'd already put on my hat and straightened my hair up in Mr. Morley's room. Some people," went on Miss Sainsbury Seale, warming to her subject, "take off their hats *downstairs* in the waiting-room, but I *never* do. A most distressing thing happened to a friend of mine who did that. It was a new hat and she put it very carefully on a chair, and when she came down, would you believe it, *a child had sat on it* and squashed it flat. Ruined! Absolutely ruined!"

"A catastrophe," said Poirot politely.

"I blame the mother entirely," said Miss Sainsbury Seale judicially. "Mothers should keep an eye on their children. The little dears do not mean any harm, but they have to be *watched*."

Japp said, "Then this young man with toothache was the only other patient you noticed at fifty-eight Queen Charlotte Street?"

"A gentleman came down the stairs and went out just as I went up to Mr. Morley— Oh, and I remember—a very *peculiar* looking foreigner came *out* of the house just as I arrived."

Japp coughed. Poirot said with dignity, "That was I, madame."

"Oh, dear!" Miss Sainsbury Seale peered at him. "So it was! Do forgive—so shortsighted—and very dark here, isn't it?" She trailed off into incoherencies. "And really, you know, I flatter myself that I have a *very* good memory for faces. But the light here *is* dim, isn't it? Do forgive my most unfortunate mistake!"

They soothed the lady down, and Japp asked, "You are quite sure Mr. Morley didn't say anything such as—for instance—that he was expecting a painful interview this morning? Anything of that kind?"

"No, indeed, I'm sure he didn't."

"He didn't mention a patient by the name of Amberiotis?"

"No, no. He really said nothing—except, I mean, the things that dentists *have* to say."

Through Poirot's mind there ran quickly, *"Rinse. Open a little wider, please. Now close gently."*

Japp had proceeded to his next step. It would possibly be necessary for Miss Sainsbury Seale to give evidence at the inquest.

After a first scream of dismay, Miss Sainsbury Seale seemed to take kindly to the idea. A tentative inquiry from

Japp produced Miss Sainsbury Seale's whole life history.

She had, it seemed, come from India to England six months ago. She had lived in various hotels and boarding-houses and had finally come to the Glengowrie Court which she liked very much because of its homely atmosphere; in India she had lived mostly in Calcutta where she had done mission work and had also taught elocution.

"Pure, well-enunciated English—most important, Chief Inspector. You see"—Miss Sainsbury Seale simpered and bridled—"as a girl I was on the stage. Oh, only in small parts, you know. The provinces! But I had great ambitions. Repertory. Then I went on a world tour—Shakespeare, Bernard Shaw." She sighed. "The trouble with us poor women is *heart*—at the mercy of our *hearts*. A rash, impulsive marriage. Alas! We parted almost immediately. I—I had been sadly deceived. I resumed my maiden name. A friend kindly provided me with a little capital and I started my elocution school. I helped to found a very good amateur dramatic society. I must show you some of our notices."

Chief Inspector Japp knew the dangers of *that!* He escaped, Miss Sainsbury Seale's last words being—"and if, by any chance, my name *should* be in the papers—as a witness at the inquest, I mean—you *will* be sure that it is spelled right? Mabelle Sainsbury Seale—Mabelle spelled M.A.B.E.L.L.E., and Seale S.E.A.L.E. And of course, if they *did* care to mention that I appeared in *As You Like It* at the Oxford Repertory Theatre—"

"Of course, of course." Chief Inspector Japp fairly fled. In the taxi, he sighed and wiped his forehead.

"If it's ever necessary, we ought to be able to check up on *her* all right," he observed, "unless it was *all* lies—but that I *don't* believe!"

Poirot shook his head.

"Liars," he said, "are neither so circumstantial nor so inconsequential."

Japp went on, "I was afraid she'd jib at the inquest—most middle-aged spinsters do—but her having been an actress accounts for her being eager. Bit of limelight for her!"

Poirot said, "Do you really want her at the inquest?"

"Probably not. It depends." He paused and then said, "I'm more than ever convinced, Poirot. *This wasn't suicide.*"

"And the motive?"

"Has us beat for the moment. Suppose Morley once seduced Amberiotis's daughter?"

Poirot was silent. He tried to visualize Mr. Morley in the role of seducer to a luscious-eyed Greek maiden, but failed lamentably.

He reminded Japp that Mr. Reilly had said his partner had had no joy of living.

Japp said vaguely, "Oh, well, you never know what may happen on a cruise!" And he added with satisfaction, "We shall know better where we stand when we've talked to this fellow."

They paid off the taxi and entered the Savoy.

Japp asked for Mr. Amberiotis.

The clerk looked at them rather oddly. He said, "Mr. Amberiotis? I'm sorry, sir, I'm afraid you can't see him."

"Oh, yes, I can, my lad," Japp said grimly. He drew the other a little aside and showed him his credentials.

The clerk said, "You don't understand, sir. *Mr. Amberiotis died half an hour ago.*"

To Hercule Poirot it was as though a door had gently but firmly shut.

Chapter Three

FIVE, SIX, PICK UP STICKS

TWENTY-FOUR HOURS LATER Japp rang Poirot up. His tone was bitter.

"Washout! The whole thing!"

"What do you mean, my friend?"

"Morley committed suicide all right. We've got the motive."

"What was it?"

"I've just had the doctor's report on Amberiotis's death. I won't give you the official jargon but in plain English he died as the result of an overdose of adrenaline and procaine. It acted on his heart, I understand, and he collapsed. When the wretched devil said he was feeling bad yesterday afternoon, he was just speaking the truth. Well, there you are! Adrenaline and procaine is the mixture dentists inject into your gums—local anesthetic. Morley made an error, injected an overdose, and then after Amberiotis left, he realized what he had done, couldn't face the music, and shot himself."

"With a pistol he was not known to possess?" queried Poirot.

"He *may* have possessed it all the same. Relations don't know everything. You'd be surprised sometimes, the things they *don't* know!"

"That is true, yes."

Japp said, "Well, there you are. It's a perfectly logical explanation of the whole thing."

Poirot said, "You know, my friend, it does not quite satisfy me. It is true that patients have been known to react unfavorably to these local anesthetics. Adrenaline idiosyncrasy is well-known. In combination with procaine toxic effects have followed quite small doses. *But* the doctor or dentist who employed the drug does not usually carry his concern as far as killing himself!"

"Yes, but you're talking of cases where the employment of the anesthetic was normal. In that case no particular blame attaches to the surgeon concerned. It is the idiosyncrasy of the patient that has caused death. But in this case it's pretty clear that there was a definite overdose. They haven't got the exact amount yet—these quantitative analyses seem to take a month of Sundays—but it was definitely more than the normal dose. That means that Morley must have made a mistake."

"Even then," said Poirot, "it *was* a mistake. It would not be a criminal matter."

"No, but it wouldn't do him any good in his profession. In fact, it would pretty well ruin him. Nobody's going to go to a dentist who's likely to shoot lethal doses of poison into you just because he happens to be a bit absent-minded."

"It was a curious thing to do, I admit."

"These things happen—they happen to doctors—they happen to chemists. Careful and reliable for years, and then—one moment's inattention—and the mischief's done and the poor devils are for it. Morley was a sensitive man. In the case of a doctor, there's usually a chemist or a dispenser to share the blame—or to shoulder it altogether. In this case Morley was solely responsible."

Poirot demurred.

"Would he not have left some message behind him, saying what he had done and that he could not face the consequences? Something of that kind? Just a word for his sister?"

"No, as I see it, he suddenly realized what had happened—and just lost his nerve and took the quickest way out."

Poirot did not answer.

Japp said, "I know you, old boy. Once you've got your teeth into a case of murder, you like it to *be* a case of murder! I admit I'm responsible for setting you on the track this time. Well, I made a mistake. I admit it freely."

Poirot said, "I still think, you know, that there might be another explanation."

"Plenty of other explanations, I daresay. I've thought of them—but they're all too fantastic. Let's say that Amberiotis shot Morley, went home, was filled with remorse, and committed suicide, using some stuff he'd pinched from Morley's surgery. If you think *that's* likely, *I* think it's damned *un*likely. We've got a record of Amberiotis at the Yard. Quite interesting. Started as a little hotelkeeper in Greece, then he mixed himself up in politics. He's done espionage work in Germany and in France—and made very pretty little sums of money. But he wasn't getting rich quick enough that way, and he's believed to have done a spot or two of blackmail. Not a nice man, our Mr. Amberiotis. He was out in India last year and is believed to have bled one of the native princes rather freely. The difficult thing has been ever to prove anything against him. Slippery as an eel! Then there is another possibility. He might have been blackmailing Morley over something or other. Morley, having a golden opportunity, plugs an overdose of adrenaline and procaine into him, hoping that the verdict will be an unfortunate accident—adrenaline idiosyncrasy—something of that sort. Then, after the man's gone away Morley gets a fit of remorse and does himself in. That's possible, of course, but I can't somehow see Morley as a deliberate murderer. No, I'm pretty sure it was what I first said—a genuine mistake, made on a morning when he was overworked. We'll have to leave it at that, Poirot. I've talked to the A.C. and he's quite clear on it."

"I see," said Poirot, with a sigh. "I see—"

Japp said kindly, "I know what you feel, old boy. But

you can't have a nice juicy murder *every* time! So long. All I can say by way of apology is the old phrase, 'Sorry you have been troubled!' "

He rang off.

Hercule Poirot sat at his handsome modern desk. He liked modern furniture. Its squareness and solidity were more agreeable to him than the soft contours of antique models.

In front of him was a square sheet of paper with neat headings and comments. Against some of them were query marks.

First came:

Amberiotis. Espionage. In England for that purpose? Was in India last year. During period of riots and unrest. Could be a Communist agent.

There was a space and then the next heading:

Frank Carter? Morley thought him unsatisfactory. Was discharged from his employment recently. Why?

After that came a name with merely a question mark:

Howard Raikes?

Next came a sentence in quotes:

"But that's absurd!" ???

Hercule Poirot's head was poised interrogatively. Outside the window a bird was carrying a twig to build its nest. Hercule Poirot looked rather like a bird as he sat there with his egg-shaped head cocked on one side.

He made another entry a little farther down.

Mr. Barnes?

He paused and then wrote:

Morley's office? Mark on carpet. Possibilities.

He considered that last entry for some time.
Then he got up, called for his hat and stick, and went out.

Three-quarters of an hour later Hercule Poirot came out of the underground station at Ealing Broadway and five minutes after that he had reached his destination—88 Castlegardens Road.

It was a small, semidetached house, and the neatness of the front garden drew an admiring nod from Hercule Poirot.

"Admirably symmetrical," he murmured to himself.

Mr. Barnes was at home and Poirot was shown into a small, precise dining-room and here presently Mr. Barnes came to him.

Mr. Barnes was a small man with twinkling eyes and a nearly bald head. He peeped over the top of his glasses at his visitor while in his left hand he twirled the card that Poirot had given the maid.

He said in a small, prim, almost falsetto voice, "Well, well, M. Poirot? I am honored, I am sure."

"You must excuse my calling upon you in this informal manner," said Poirot punctiliously.

"Much the best way," said Mr. Barnes. "And the time is admirable, too. A quarter to seven—very sound time at this period of the year for catching anyone at home." He waved his hand. "Sit down, M. Poirot. I've no doubt we've got a good deal to talk about. Number fifty-eight Queen Charlotte Street, I suppose?"

Poirot said, "You suppose rightly—but why should you

suppose anything of the kind?"

"My dear sir," said Mr. Barnes, "I've been retired from the Home Office for some time now—but I've not gone *quite* rusty yet. If there's any hush-hush business, it's far better not to use the police. Draws attention to it all!"

Poirot said, "I will ask yet another question. Why should you suppose this is a hush-hush business?"

"Isn't it?" asked the other. "Well, if it isn't, in my opinion it ought to be." He leaned forward and tapped with his pince-nez on the arm of the chair. "In secret service work it's never the little fry you want—it's the big bugs at the top—but to get them you've got to be careful not to alarm the little fry."

"It seems to me, Mr. Barnes, that you know more than I do," said Hercule Poirot.

"Don't know anything at all," replied the other. "Just put two and two together."

"One of those two being?"

"Amberiotis," said Mr. Barnes promptly. "You forget I sat opposite to him in the waiting-room for a minute or two. *He* didn't know *me*. I was always an insignificant chap. Not a bad thing sometimes. But I knew *him* all right —and I could guess what he was up to over here."

"Which was?"

Mr. Barnes twinkled more than ever.

"We're very tiresome people in this country. We're conservative, you know, conservative to the backbone. We grumble a lot, but we don't really want to smash our democratic government and try new-fangled experiments. That's what's so heartbreaking to the wretched foreign agitator who's working full time and over! The whole trouble is—from their point of view—that we really *are*, as a country, comparatively solvent. Hardly any other country in Europe is at the moment! To upset England— really upset it—you've got to play hell with its finance— that's what it comes to! And you can't play hell with its finance when you've got men like Alistair Blunt at the helm."

Mr. Barnes paused and then went on. "Blunt is the kind of man who in private life would always pay his bills and live within his income—whether he'd got twopence a year or several million makes no difference. He is that type of fellow. And he just simply thinks that there's no reason why a *country* shouldn't do the same! No costly experiments. No frenzied expenditure on possible Utopias. That's why—" he paused "—that's why certain people have made up their minds that Blunt must go."

"Ah," said Poirot.

Mr. Barnes nodded.

"Yes," he said. "I know what I'm talking about. Quite nice people, some of 'em. Long-haired, earnest-eyed, and full of ideals of a better world. Others not so nice, rather nasty in fact. Furtive little rats with beards and foreign accents. And another lot again of the big bully type. But they've all got the same idea: Blunt must go!"

He tilted his chair gently back and forward again.

"Sweep away the old order! The Tories, the Conservatives, the die-hards, the hard-headed suspicious businessmen, that's the idea. Perhaps these people are right—*I* don't know—but I know one thing—you've got to have something to put in the place of the old order—something that will work—not just something that *sounds* all right. Well, we needn't go into that. We're dealing with concrete facts, not abstract theories. Take away the props and the building will come down. Blunt is one of the props of Things as They Are."

He leaned forward.

"*They're out after Blunt all right.* That I *know*. And it's my opinion that yesterday morning *they nearly got him.* I may be wrong—but it's been tried before. The method, I mean."

He paused and then quietly, circumspectly, he mentioned three names. An unusually able Chancellor of the Exchequer, a progressive and far-sighted manufacturer, and a hopeful young politician who had captured the public fancy. The first had died on the operating table, the second had succumbed to an obscure disease which had been recognized too late, the third had been run down by a car and killed.

"It's very easy," said Mr. Barnes. "The anesthetist muffed the giving of the anesthetic—well, that does happen. In the second case the symptoms were puzzling. The doctor was just a well meaning G.P., couldn't be expected to recognize them. In the third case, anxious mother was driving car in a hurry to get to her sick child. Sob stuff— the jury acquitted her of blame!"

He paused. "All quite natural. And soon forgotten. But I'll just tell you *where those three people are now*. The anesthetist is set up on his own with a first-class research laboratory—no expense spared. That G.P. has retired from practice. He's got a yacht, and a nice little place on the Broads. The mother is giving all her children a first-class education, ponies to ride in the holidays, nice house in the country with a big garden and paddocks."

He nodded his head slowly.

"In every profession and walk of life there is *someone* who is vulnerable to temptation. The trouble in our case was that Morley *wasn't!*"

"You think it was like that?" said Hercule Poirot.

Mr. Barnes said, "I do. It's not easy to get at one of these big men, you know. They're fairly well protected. The car stunt is risky and doesn't always succeed. But a man is defenseless enough in a dentist's chair."

He took off his pince-nez, polished them, and put them on again. He said, "That's my theory! *Morley wouldn't do the job*. He knew too much, though, so they had to put him out."

"*They?*" asked Poirot.

"When I say *they*—I mean the organization that's behind all this. Only one person actually did the job, of course."

"Which person?"

"Well, I could make a guess," said Mr. Barnes, "but it's only a guess and I might be wrong."

Poirot said quietly, "Reilly?"

"Of course! He's the obvious person. I think that probably they never asked Morley to do the job *himself*. What he *was* to do, was to turn Blunt over to his partner at the last minute. Sudden illness, something of that sort. Reilly would have done the actual business—and there would have been another regrettable accident—death of a famous banker—unhappy young dentist in court in such a state of dither and misery that he would have been let down lightly. He'd have given up dentistry afterward—and settled down somewhere on a nice income of several thousands a year."

Mr. Barnes looked across at Poirot.

"Don't think I'm romancing," he said. "These things happen."

"Yes, yes, I know they happen."

Mr. Barnes went on, tapping a book with a lurid jacket that lay on a table close at hand.

"I read a lot of these spy yarns. Fantastic, some of them. But curiously enough *they're not any more fantastic than the real thing*. There *are* beautiful adventuresses, and dark sinister men with foreign accents, and gangs and international associations and supercrooks! I'd blush to see some of the things *I* know set down in print—nobody would believe them for a minute!"

Poirot said, "In your theory, *where does Amberiotis come in?*"

"I'm not quite sure. I *think* he was meant to take the rap. He's played a double game more than once and I daresay he was framed. That's only an idea, mind."

Hercule Poirot said quietly, "Granting that your ideas are correct—*what will happen next?*"

Mr. Barnes rubbed his nose.

"They'll try to get him again," he said. "Oh, yes. They'll have another try. Time's short. Blunt has got people looking after him, I daresay. They'll have to be extra careful. It won't be a man hiding in a bush with a pistol. Nothing so crude as that. You tell 'em to look out for the respectable people—the relations, the old servants, the chemist's assistant who makes up a medicine, the wine merchant who sells him his port. Getting Alistair Blunt out of the way is worth a great many millions, and it's wonderful what people will do for—say, a nice little income of four thousand a year!"

"As much as that?"

"Possibly more—"

Poirot was silent a moment, then he said, "I have had Reilly in mind from the first."

"Irish? I.R.A.?"

"Not that so much but there was a mark, you see, on the carpet, as though the body had been dragged along it. But if Morley was shot by a patient he would be shot in the surgery and there would be no need to move the body. That is why, from the first, I suspected that he had been shot, not in the surgery, but in his office—next door. That would mean that it was not a patient who shot him, but some member of his own household."

"Neat," said Mr. Barnes appreciatively.

Hercule Poirot got up and held out a hand. "Thank you," he said. "You have helped me a great deal."

On his way home, Poirot called in at the Glengowrie Court Hotel.

As a result of that visit he rang up Japp very early the following morning.

"*Bonjour, mon ami.* The inquest is today, is it not?"

"It is. Are you going to attend?"

"I do not think so."

"It won't really be worth your while, I expect."

"Are you calling Miss Sainsbury Seale as a witness?"

"The lovely Mabelle—why can't she just spell it plain Mabel? These women get my goat! No, I'm not calling her. There's no need."

"You have heard nothing from her?"

"No, why should I?"

Hercule Poirot said, "I wondered, that was all. Perhaps it may interest you to learn that Miss Sainsbury Seale walked out of the Glengowrie Court Hotel just before dinner the night before last—and did not come back."

"*What?* She's hooked it?"

"That is a possible explanation."

"But why should she? She's quite all right, you know. Perfectly genuine and aboveboard. I cabled to Calcutta about her—that was before I knew the reason for Amberiotis's death, otherwise I shouldn't have bothered—and I got the reply last night. Everything okay. She's been known there for years, and her whole account of herself is true—except that she slurred over her marriage a bit. Married a Hindu student and then found he'd got a few attachments already. So she resumed her maiden name and took to good works. She's hand in gloves with the missionaries—teaches elocution and helps in amateur dramatic shows. In fact, what I call a terrible woman—but definitely above suspicion of being mixed up in a murder. And *now* you say she's walked out on us! I can't understand it." He paused a minute and then went on doubtfully. "Perhaps she just got fed up with that hotel? I could have easily."

Poirot said, "Her luggage is still there. She took nothing with her."

Japp swore.

"When did she go?"

"About a quarter to seven."

"What about the hotel people?"

"They're very upset. Manageress looked quite distraught."

"Why didn't they report to the police?"

"Because, *mon cher,* supposing that a lady does happen to stay out for a night (however unlikely it may seem from her appearance) she will be justifiably annoyed by finding on her return that the police have been called in. Mrs. Harrison, the manageress in question, called up various hospitals in case there had been an accident. She was considering notifying the police when I called. My appearance seemed to her like an answer to prayer. I charged myself with everything, and explained that I would enlist the help of a very discreet police officer."

"The discreet police officer being yours truly, I suppose?"

"You suppose rightly."

Japp groaned.

"All right. I'll meet you at the Glengowrie Court Hotel after the inquest."

Japp grumbled as they were waiting for the manageress. "What does the woman want to disappear for?"

"It is curious, you admit?"

They had no time for more.

Mrs. Harrison, proprietor of the Glengowrie Court, was with them.

Mrs. Harrison was voluble and almost tearful. She was so worried about Miss Sainsbury Seale. What *could* have happened to her? Rapidly she went over every possibility of disaster. Loss of memory, sudden illness, hemorrhage, run down by an omnibus, robbery and assault—

She paused at last for breath, murmuring, "Such a nice type of woman—and she seemed so happy and comfortable here."

She took them, at Japp's request, up to the chaste bedroom occupied by the missing lady. Everything was neat and orderly. Clothes hung in the wardrobe, nightclothes were folded ready on the bed, in a corner were Miss Sainsbury Seale's two modest suitcases. A row of shoes stood under the dressing-table—some serviceable Oxfords, two pairs of rather meretricious glacé fancy shoes with court heels and ornamented with bows of leather, some plain black satin evening shoes, practically new, and a pair of moccasins. Poirot noted that the evening shoes were a size smaller than the day ones—a fact that might be put down to corns or to vanity. He wondered whether Miss Sainsbury Seale had found time to sew the second buckle on her shoe before she went out. He hoped so. Slovenliness in dress always annoyed him.

Japp was busy looking through some letters in a drawer of the dressing-table. Hercule Poirot gingerly pulled open a drawer of the chest of drawers. It was full of underclothing. He shut it again modestly, murmuring that Miss Sainsbury Scale seemed to believe in wearing wool next the skin, and opened another drawer which contained stockings.

Japp said, "Got anything, Poirot?"

Poirot said sadly, as he dangled a pair, "Nine inch, cheap shiny silk, price probably 2/11."

Japp said, "You're not valuing for probate, old boy. Two letters here from India, one or two receipts from charitable organizations, no bills. Most estimable character, our Miss Sainsbury Seale."

"But very little taste in dress," said Poirot sadly.

"Probably thought dress worldly." Japp was noting down an address from an old letter dated two months back.

"These people may know something about her," he said. "Address up Hampstead way. Sound as though they were fairly intimate."

There was nothing more to be gleaned at the Glengowrie Court Hotel except the negative fact that Miss Sainsbury Seale had not seemed excited or worried in any way when she went out, and it would appear that she had definitely intended to return since, on passing her friend Mrs. Bolitho in the hall, she had called out, "After dinner I will show you that patience I was telling you about."

Moreover, it was the custom at the Glengowrie Court to give notice in the dining-room if you intended to be out for a meal. Miss Sainsbury Seale had not done so. Therefore, it seemed clear that she had intended returning for dinner which was served from seven-thirty to eight-thirty.

But she had not returned. She had walked out into the Cromwell Road and disappeared.

Japp and Poirot called at the address in West Hampstead which had headed the letter found.

It was a pleasant house and the Adamses were pleasant people with a large family. They had lived in India for many years and spoke warmly of Miss Sainsbury Seale. But they could not help.

They had not seen her lately, not for a month, in fact, not since they came back from their Easter holidays. She had been staying then at a hotel near Russell Square. Mrs. Adams gave Poirot the address of it and also the address of some other Anglo-Indian friends of Miss Sainsbury Seale's who lived in Streatham.

But the two men drew a blank in both places. Miss Sainsbury Seale had stayed at the hotel in question, but they remembered very little about her and nothing that could be of any help. She was a nice quiet lady and had lived abroad. The people in Streatham were no help, either. They had not seen Miss Sainsbury Seale since February.

There remained the possibility of an accident, but that possibility was dispelled, too. No hospital had admitted any casualty answering to the description given.

Miss Sainsbury Seale had disappeared into space.

On the following morning, Poirot went to the Holborn Palace Hotel and asked for Mr. Howard Raikes.

By this time it would hardly have surprised him to hear that Mr. Howard Raikes, too, had stepped out one evening and had never returned.

Mr. Howard Raikes, however, was still at the Holborn Palace and was said to be breakfasting.

The apparition of Hercule Poirot at the breakfast table seemed to give Mr. Raikes doubtful pleasure.

Though not looking so murderous as in Poirot's disordered recollection of him, his scowl was still formidable —he stared at his uninvited guest and said ungraciously, "What the hell?"

"You permit?"

Hercule Poirot drew a chair from another table.

Mr. Raikes said, "Don't mind me! Sit down and make yourself at home!"

Poirot smilingly availed himself of the permission.

Mr. Raikes said ungraciously, "Well, what do you want?"

"Do you remember me at all, Mr. Raikes?"

"Never set eyes on you in my life."

"There you are wrong. You sat in the same room with me for at least five minutes not more than three days ago."

"I can't remember everyone I meet at some goddamned party or other."

"It was not a party," said Poirot. "It was a dentist's waiting-room."

Some swift emotion flashed into the young man's eyes and died again at once. His manner changed. It was no longer impatient and casual. It became suddenly wary. He looked across at Poirot and said, "Well?"

Poirot studied him carefully before replying. He felt,

quite positively, that this was indeed a dangerous young man. A lean, hungry face, an aggressive jaw, the eyes of a fanatic. It was a face, though, that women might find attractive. He was untidily, even shabbily dressed, and he ate with a careless voraciousness that was, so the man watching him thought, significant.

Poirot summed him up to himself. *It is a wolf with ideas—*

Raikes said harshly, "What the hell do you mean—coming here like this?"

"My visit is disagreeable to you?"

"I don't even know who you are."

"I apologize."

Dexterously Poirot whipped out his cardcase. He extracted a card and passed it across the table.

Again that emotion that he could not quite define showed upon Mr. Raikes's lean face. It was not fear—it was more aggressive than fear. After it, quite unquestionably, came anger.

He tossed the card back.

"So that's who you are, is it? I've heard of you."

"Most people have," said Hercule Poirot modestly.

"You're a private dick, aren't you? The expensive kind. The kind people hire when money is no object—when it's worth paying anything in order to save their miserable skins!"

"If you do not drink your coffee," said Hercule Poirot, "it will get cold."

He spoke kindly and with authority.

Raikes stared at him.

"Say, just what kind of an insect are you?"

"The coffee in this country is very bad anyway—" said Poirot.

"I'll say it is," agreed Mr. Raikes with fervor.

"But if you allow it to get cold it is practically undrinkable."

The young man leaned forward.

"What are you getting at? What's the big idea in coming round here?"

Poirot shrugged his shoulders.

"I wanted to—see you."

"Oh, yes?" said Mr. Raikes skeptically.

His eyes narrowed.

"If it's money you're after, you've come to the wrong man! The people I'm in with can't afford to *buy* what they want. Better go back to the man who pays you your salary."

Poirot said, sighing, "Nobody has paid me anything—yet."

"You're telling me," said Mr. Raikes.

"It is the truth," said Hercule Poirot. "I am wasting a good deal of valuable time for no recompense whatsoever. Simply, shall we say, to assuage my curiosity."

"And I suppose," said Mr. Raikes, "you were just assuaging your curiosity at that darned dentist's the other day."

Poirot shook his head. He said, "You seem to overlook the most ordinary reason for being in a dentist's waiting-room—which is that one is waiting to have one's teeth attended to."

"So that's what you were doing?" Mr. Raikes's tone expressed contemptuous unbelief. "Waiting to have your teeth seen to?"

"Certainly."

"You'll excuse me if I say I don't believe it."

"May I ask then, Mr. Raikes, what *you* were doing there?"

Mr. Raikes grinned suddenly. He said, "Got you there! I was waiting to have my teeth seen to also."

"You had perhaps the toothache?"

"That's right, big boy."

"But all the same, you went away without having your

teeth attended to?"

"What if I did? That's my business."

He paused—then he said, with a quick savagery of tone, "Oh, what the hell's the use of all this slick talking? You were there to look after your big shot. Well, he's all right, isn't he? Nothing happened to your precious Mr. Alistair Blunt. You've nothing on me."

Poirot said, "Where did you go when you went so abruptly out of the waiting-room?"

"Left the house, of course."

"Ah!" Poirot looked up at the ceiling. "But nobody saw you leave, Mr. Raikes."

"Does that matter?"

"It might. Somebody died in that house not long afterward, remember."

Raikes said carelessly, "Oh, you mean the dentist fellow."

Poirot's tone was hard as he said, "Yes, I mean the dentist fellow."

Raikes stared. He said, "You trying to pin that on me? Is that the game? Well, you can't do it. I've just read the account of the inquest yesterday. The poor devil shot himself because he'd made a mistake with a local anesthetic and one of his patients died."

Poirot went on unmoved. "Can you prove that you left the house when you say you did? Is there anyone who can say definitely where you were between twelve and one?"

The other's eyes narrowed.

"So you *are* trying to pin it on me? I suppose Blunt put you up to this?"

Poirot sighed. He said, "You will pardon me, but it seems an obsession with you—this persistent harping on Mr. Alistair Blunt. I am not employed by him, I never have been employed by him. I am concerned, not with his safety, but with the death of a man who did good work in his chosen profession."

Raikes shook his head.

"Sorry," he said. "I don't believe you. You're Blunt's private dick all right." His face hardened as he leaned across the table. "But you can't save him, you know. He's got to go—he and everything he stands for! There's got to be a new deal—the old corrupt system of finance has got to go—this cursed net of bankers all over the world like a spider's web. They've got to be swept away. I've nothing against Blunt personally—but he's the type of man I hate. He's mediocre—he's smug. He's the sort you can't move unless you use dynamite. He's the sort of man who says, 'You can't disrupt the foundations of civilization.' Can't you, though? Let him wait and see! He's an obstruction in the way of progress and he's got to be removed. There's no room in the world today for men like Blunt—men who hark back to the past—men who want to live as their fathers lived or even as their grandfathers lived! You've got a lot of them here in England—crusted old die-hards—useless, worn-out symbols of a decayed era. And my God, they've got to go! There's got to be a new world. Do you get me—a new world, see?"

Poirot sighed and rose. He said, "I see, Mr. Raikes, that you are an idealist."

"What if I am?"

"Too much of an idealist to care about the death of a dentist."

Mr. Raikes said scornfully, "What does the death of one miserable dentist matter?"

Hercule Poirot said, "It does not matter to you. It matters to me. That is the difference between us."

Poirot arrived home to be informed by George that a lady was waiting to see him.

"She is—ahem—a little nervous, sir," said George.

Since the lady had given no name Poirot was at liberty to guess. He guessed wrong, for the young woman who rose agitatedly from the sofa as he entered was the late Mr. Morley's secretary, Miss Gladys Nevill.

"Oh, dear, M. Poirot. I am *so* sorry to worry you like this—and really I don't know how I had the courage to come—I'm afraid you'll think it very bold of me—and I'm sure I don't want to take up your time—I know what time means to a busy professional man—but really I have been so unhappy—only I daresay you will think it all a waste of time—"

Profiting by a long experience of the English people, Poirot suggested a cup of tea. Miss Nevill's reaction was all that could be hoped for.

"Well, really, M. Poirot, that's *very* kind of you. Not that it's so very long since breakfast, but one can always do with a cup of tea, can't one?"

Poirot, who could always do without one, assented mendaciously. George was instructed to this effect and in a miraculously short time, Poirot and his visitor faced each other across a tea tray.

"I must apologize to you," said Miss Nevill, regaining her usual aplomb under the influence of the beverage, "but as a matter of fact the inquest yesterday upset me a good deal."

"I'm sure it must have," said Poirot kindly.

"There was no question of my giving evidence, or anything like *that*. But I felt somebody *ought* to go with Miss Morley. Mr. Reilly was there, of course—but I meant a *woman*. Besides, Miss Morley doesn't *like* Mr. Reilly. So I thought it was my duty to go."

"That was very kind of you," said Poirot, encouragingly.

"Oh, no, I just felt I *had* to. You see, I have worked for Mr. Morley for quite a number of years now—and the whole thing was a great shock to me—and, of course, the inquest made it worse—"

"I'm afraid it must have."

Miss Nevill leaned forward earnestly.

"*But it's all wrong, M. Poirot. It really is all wrong.*"

"What is wrong, mademoiselle?"

"Well, it just couldn't have happened—not the way they make out—giving a patient an overdose in injecting the gum, I mean."

"You think not."

"I'm sure about it. Occasionally patients do suffer ill effects, but that is because they are physiologically unfit subjects—their heart action isn't normal. But I'm sure that an overdose is a very rare thing. You see practitioners get so into the habit of giving the regulation amount that it is absolutely mechanical—they'd give the right dose automatically."

Poirot nodded approvingly. He said, "That is what I thought myself, yes."

"It's so standardized, you see. It's not like a chemist who is making up different amounts the whole time, or multiplying dosage, where an error might creep in through inattention. Or a doctor who writes a great many different prescriptions. But a dentist isn't like that at all."

Poirot asked, "You did not ask to be allowed to make these observations in the coroner's court?"

Gladys Nevill shook her head. She twisted her fingers uncertainly.

"You see," she broke out at last, "I was afraid of—of making things worse. Of course *I* know that Mr. Morley wouldn't do such a thing—but it might make people think that he—that he had done it deliberately."

Poirot nodded.

Gladys Nevill said, "That's why I came to you, M. Poirot. Because with you it—it wouldn't be *official* in any way. But I do think *somebody* ought to know how—how *unconvincing* the whole thing is."

"Nobody wants to know," said Poirot.

She stared at him, puzzled.

Poirot said, "I should like to know a little more about that telegram you received, summoning you away that day."

"Honestly, I don't know what to think about that, M. Poirot. It does seem so queer. You see, it must have been sent by someone who knew all about me—and Aunt—where she lived and everything."

"Yes, it would seem as though it must have been sent by one of your intimate friends, or by someone who lived in the house and knew all about you."

"None of my friends would do such a thing, M. Poirot."

"You have no ideas yourself on the subject?"

The girl hesitated. She said slowly, "Just at first, when I realized that Mr. Morley had shot himself, I wondered if he could possibly have sent it."

"You mean, out of consideration for you, to get you out of the way?"

The girl nodded.

"But that really seemed a fantastic idea, even if he *had* got the idea of suicide in his mind that morning. It's really very odd. Frank—my friend, you know—was quite absurd at first about it. He accused me of wanting to go off for the day with somebody else—as though I would do such a thing."

"Is there a somebody else?"

Miss Nevill blushed.

"No, of course there isn't. But Frank has been so different lately—so moody and suspicious. Really, you know, it was losing his job and not being able to get another. Just hanging about is so bad for a man. I've been very worried about Frank."

"He was upset, was he not, to find you had gone away that day?"

"Yes; you see, he came round to tell me he had got a new job—a marvelous job—ten pounds a week. And he couldn't wait. He wanted me to know right away. And I think he wanted Mr. Morley to know, too, because he'd been very hurt at the way Mr. Morley didn't appreciate him, and he suspected Mr. Morley of trying to influence me against him."

"Which was true, was it not?"

"Well, yes, it was, in a *way!* Of course, Frank *has* lost a good many jobs and he hasn't been, perhaps, what most people would call very *steady*. But it will be different now. I think one can do so much by influence, don't you, M. Poirot? If a man feels a woman expects a lot of him, he tries to live up to her ideal of him."

Poirot sighed. But he did not argue. He had heard many hundreds of women produce that same argument, with the same blithe belief in the redeeming power of a woman's love. Once in a thousand times, he supposed, cynically, it *might* be true.

He merely said, "I should like to meet this friend of yours."

"I'd love to have you meet him, M. Poirot. But just at present Sunday is his only free day. He's away in the country all the week, you see."

"Ah, on the new job. What is the job, by the way?"

"Well, I don't exactly know, M. Poirot. Something in the secretarial line, I imagine. Or some government department. I know I have to send letters to Frank's London address and they get forwarded."

"That is a little odd, is it not?"

"Well, I thought so—but Frank says it is often done nowadays."

Poirot looked at her for a moment or two without speaking.

Then he said deliberately, "Tomorrow is Sunday, is it not? Perhaps you would both give me the pleasure of lunching with me—at Logan's Corner House? I should like to discuss this sad business with you both."

"Well—thank you, M. Poirot. I—yes, I'm sure we'd like to lunch with you very much."

Frank Carter was a fair young man of medium height. His appearance was cheaply smart. He talked readily and fluently. His eyes were set rather close together and they had a way of shifting uneasily from side to side when he was embarrassed.

He was inclined to be suspicious and slightly hostile.

"I'd no idea we were to have the pleasure of lunching with *you*, M. Poirot. Gladys didn't tell me anything about it."

He shot her a rather annoyed glance as he spoke.

"It was only arranged yesterday," said Poirot, smiling. "Miss Nevill is very upset by the circumstances of Mr. Morley's death and I wondered if we put our heads together—"

Frank Carter interrupted him rudely.

"Morley's death? I'm sick of Morley's death! Why can't you forget him, Gladys? There wasn't anything so wonderful about him that *I* can see."

"Oh, Frank, I don't think you ought to say *that*. Why, he left me a hundred pounds. I got the letter about it last night."

"That's all right," admitted Frank grudgingly. "But after all, why shouldn't he? He worked you like a nigger—and who pocketed all the fat fees? Why, he did!"

"Well, of course he did—he paid me a very good salary."

"Not according to *my* ideas! You're too humble altogether, Gladys, my girl, you let yourself be put upon, you know. *I* sized Morley up all right. You know as well as I do that he tried his best to get you to give me the chuck."

"He didn't understand."

"He understood all right. The man's dead now—otherwise I can tell you I'd have given him a piece of my mind."

"You actually came round to do so on the morning of

his death, did you not?" Hercule Poirot inquired gently.

Frank Carter said angrily, "Who's been saying so?"

"You did come round, did you not?"

"What if I did? I wanted to see Miss Nevill here."

"But they told you she was away."

"Yes, and that made me pretty suspicious, I can tell you. I told that redheaded oaf I'd wait and see Morley myself. This business of putting Gladys against me had gone on long enough. I meant to tell Morley that instead of being a poor unemployed rotter, I'd landed a good job and that it was about time Gladys handed in her notice and thought about her trousseau."

"But you did not actually tell him so?"

"No, I got tired of waiting in that dingy mausoleum I went away."

"What time did you leave?"

"I can't remember."

"What time did you arrive then?"

"I don't know. Soon after twelve, I should imagine."

"And you stayed half an hour—or longer—or less than half an hour?"

"I don't know, I tell you. I'm not the sort of chap who's always looking at a clock."

"Was there anyone in the waiting-room while you were there?"

"There was an oily fat bloke when I went in, but he wasn't there long. After that I was alone."

"Then you must have left before half-past twelve—for at that time a lady arrived."

"Daresay I did. The place got on my nerves as I tell you."

Poirot eyed him thoughtfully.

The bluster was uneasy—it did not ring quite true. And yet that might be explained by mere nervousness.

Poirot's manner was simple and friendly as he said, "Miss Nevill tells me that you have been very fortunate and have found a very good job indeed."

"The pay's good."

"Ten pounds a week, she tells me."

"That's right. Not too dusty, is it? Shows I can pull it off when I set my mind to it."

He swaggered a little.

"Yes, indeed. And the work is not too arduous?"

Frank Carter said shortly, "Not too bad."

"And interesting?"

"Oh, yes, quite interesting. Talking of jobs, I've always been interested to know how you private detectives go about things? I suppose there's not much of the Sherlock Holmes touch really? Mostly divorce nowadays?"

"I do not concern myself with divorce."

"Really? Then I don't see how you live."

"I manage, my friend, I manage."

"But you're right at the top of the tree, aren't you, M. Poirot?" put in Gladys Nevill. "Mr. Morley used to say so. I mean you're the sort of person royalty calls in, or the Home Office or duchesses."

Poirot smiled upon her.

"You flatter me," he said.

Poirot walked home through the deserted streets in a thoughtful frame of mind.

When he got in, he rang up Japp.

"Forgive my troubling you, my friend, but did you ever do anything in the matter of tracing that telegram that was sent to Gladys Nevill?"

"Still harping on the subject? Yes, we did, as a matter of fact. There was a telegram and—rather clever—the aunt lives at Richbourne in Somerset. The telegram was handed in at Richbarn—you know, the London suburb."

Hercule Poirot said appreciatively, "That was clever— yes, that was clever. If the recipient happened to glance at where the telegram was handed in, the word would look sufficiently like Richbourne to carry conviction."

He paused.

"Do you know what I think, Japp?"

"Well?"

"There are signs of brains in this business."

"Hercule Poirot wants it to be murder, so it's got to be murder."

"How do you explain that telegram?"

"Coincidence. Someone was hoaxing the girl."

"Why should they?"

"Oh, my goodness, Poirot, why do people do things? Practical jokes, hoaxes. Misplaced sense of humor, that's all."

"And somebody felt like being funny just on the day that Morley was going to make a mistake over an injection."

"There may have been a certain amount of cause and effect. Because Miss Nevill was away, Morley was more rushed than usual and consequently was more likely to make a mistake."

"I am still not satisfied."

"I daresay—but don't you see where your view is leading you? If anybody got la Nevill out of the way, it was probably Morley himself, making his killing of Amberiotis deliberate and not an accident."

Poirot was silent. Japp said, "You see?"

Poirot said, "Amberiotis might have been killed some other way."

"Not he. Nobody came to see him at the Savoy. He lunched up in his room. And the doctors say the stuff was definitely injected, not taken by mouth—it wasn't in the stomach. So there you are. It's a clear case."

"That is what we are meant to think."

"The A.C. is satisfied anyway."

"And he is satisfied with the disappearing lady?"

"The Case of the Vanishing Scal? No, I can tell you,

we're still working on that. That woman's got to be somewhere. You can't just walk out into the street and disappear."

"She seems to have done so."

"For the moment. But she must be somewhere, alive or
dead, and I don't think she is dead."

"Why not?"

"Because we'd have found her body by now."

"Oh, my Japp, do bodies always come to light so soon?"

"I suppose you're hinting that *she's* been murdered now
and that we'll find her in a quarry, cut up in little pieces
like Mrs. Ruxton?"

"After all, *mon ami,* you *do* have missing persons who
are found."

"Very seldom, old boy. Lots of women disappear, yes,
but we usually find 'em, all right. Nine times out of ten
it's a case of good old sex. They're somewhere with a man.
But I don't think it could be that with our Mabelle, do
you?"

"One never knows," said Poirot cautiously. "But I do
not think it likely. So you are sure of finding her?"

"We'll find her all right. We're publishing a description
of her to the press and we're roping in the B.B.C."

"Ah," said Poirot, "I fancy that may bring develop-
ments."

"Don't worry, old boy. We'll find your missing beauty
for you—woolen underwear and all."

He rang off.

George entered the room with his usual noiseless tread.
He set down on a little table a steaming pot of chocolate
and some sugar biscuits.

"Will there be anything else, sir?"

"I am in great perplexity of mind, George."

"Indeed, sir? I am sorry to hear it."

Hercule Poirot poured himself out some chocolate and
stirred it thoughtfully.

George stood deferentially waiting, recognizing the signs. There were moments when Hercule Poirot discussed his cases with his valet. He always said that he found George's comments singularly helpful.

"You are aware, no doubt, George, of the death of my dentist?"

"Mr. Morley, sir? Yes, sir. Very distressing, sir. He shot himself, I understand."

"That is the general understanding. If he did not shoot himself, he was murdered."

"Yes, sir."

"The question is, if he was murdered, who murdered him?"

"Quite so, sir."

"There are only a certain number of people, George, who *could* have murdered him. That is to say the people who were actually in, or *could have been in* the house at the time."

"Quite so, sir."

"Those people are: a cook and a housemaid, amiable domestics and highly unlikely to do anything of the kind. A devoted sister, also highly unlikely, but who does inherit her brother's money such as it is—and one can never entirely neglect the financial aspect. An able and efficient partner—no motive known. A somewhat boneheaded page boy addicted to cheap crime stories. And lastly, a Greek gentleman of somewhat doubtful antecedents."

George coughed.

"These foreigners, sir—"

"Exactly. I agree perfectly. The Greek gentleman is decidedly indicated. But you see, George, the Greek gentleman also died and apparently it was Mr. Morley who killed him—whether by intention or as the result of an unfortunate error we cannot be sure."

"It might be, sir, that they killed each other. I mean, sir, each gentleman had formed the idea of doing the other gentleman in, though, of course, each gentleman was unaware of the other gentleman's intention."

Hercule Poirot purred approvingly.

"Very ingenious, George. The dentist murders the unfortunate gentleman who sits in the chair, not realizing that the said victim is at that moment meditating exactly at what moment to whip out his pistol. It could, of course, be so, but it seems to me, George, extremely unlikely. And we have not come to the end of our list yet. There are still two other people who might possibly have been in the house at the given moment. Every patient before Mr. Amberiotis was actually seen to leave the house with the exception of one—a young American gentleman. He left the waiting-room at about twenty minutes to twelve, but no one actually saw him leave the house. We must, therefore, count him as a possibility. The other possibility is a certain Mr. Frank Carter (*not* a patient) who came to the house at a little after twelve with the intention of seeing Mr. Morley. Nobody saw *him* leave, either. Those, my good George, are the facts; what do you think of them?"

"At what time was the murder committed, sir?"

"If the murder was committed by Mr. Amberiotis, it was committed at any time between twelve and five and twenty past. If by somebody else, it was committed *after* twenty-five minutes past twelve, as otherwise Mr. Amberiotis would have noticed the corpse."

He looked encouragingly at George.

"Now, my good George, what have you to say about the matter?"

George pondered. He said, "It strikes me, sir—"

"Yes, George?"

"You will have to find another dentist to attend to your teeth in future, sir."

Hercule Poirot said, "You surpass yourself, George. That aspect of the matter had not as yet occurred to me!"

Looking gratified, George left the room.

Hercule Poirot remained sipping his chocolate and going over the facts he had just outlined. He felt satisfied that they were as he had stated them. Within that circle of persons was the hand that had actually done the deed— no matter whose the inspiration had been.

Then his eyebrows shot up as he realized that the list was incomplete. He had left out one name.

And no one must be left out—not even the most unlikely person.

There had been one other person in the house at the time of the murder.

He wrote down, *Mr. Barnes.*

George announced, "A lady to speak to you on the telephone, sir."

A week ago, Poirot had guessed wrongly the identity of a visitor. This time his guess was right.

He recognized the voice at once.

"M. Hercule Poirot?"

"Speaking."

"This is Jane Olivera—Mr. Alistair Blunt's niece."

"Yes, Miss Olivera."

"Could you come to the Gothic House, please? There is something I feel you ought to know."

"Certainly. What time would be convenient?"

"At six-thirty, please."

"I will be there."

For a moment the autocratic note wavered.

"I—I hope I am not interrupting your work?"

"Not at all. I was expecting you to call me."

He put down the receiver quickly. He moved away from it smiling. He wondered what excuse Jane Olivera had found for summoning him.

On arrival at the Gothic House he was shown straight into the big library overlooking the river. Alistair Blunt was sitting at the writing-table playing absent-mindedly with a paper knife. He had the slightly harassed look of a man whose womenfolk have been too much for him.

Jane Olivera was standing by the mantelpiece. A plump middle-aged woman was speaking fretfully as Poirot entered—"and I really think *my* feelings should be considered in the matter, Alistair."

"Yes, Julia, of course, of course."

Alistair Blunt spoke soothingly as he rose to greet Poirot.

"And if you're going to talk horrors I shall leave the room," added the good lady.

"I should, Mother," said Jane Olivera.

Mrs. Olivera swept from the room without condescending to take any notice of Poirot.

Alistair Blunt said, "It's very good of you to come, M. Poirot. You've met Miss Olivera, I think? It was she who sent for you—"

Jane said abruptly, "It's about this missing woman that the papers are full of. Miss Something Seale."

"Sainsbury Seale? Yes?"

"It's such a pompous name, that's why I remember. Shall I tell him, or will you, Uncle Alistair?"

"My dear, it's your story."

Jane turned once more to Poirot.

"It mayn't be important in the least—but I thought you ought to know."

"Yes?"

"It was the last time Uncle Alistair went to the dentist's—I don't mean the other day—I mean about three months ago. I went with him to Queen Charlotte Street in the Rolls and it was to take me on to some friends in Regent's Park and come back for him. We stopped at Number fifty-eight, and Uncle got out, and just as he did, a woman came out of Number fifty-eight—a middle-aged woman with fussy hair and rather arty clothes. She made a beeline for Uncle and said (Jane Olivera's voice rose to an affected squeak) , 'Oh, Mr. Blunt, you don't remember *me,* I'm *sure!*' Well, of course, I could see by Uncle's face that he *didn't* remember her in the slightest—"

Alistair Blunt sighed.

"I never do. People are always saying it—"

"He put on his special face," went on Jane. "I know it well. Kind of polite and make-believe. It wouldn't deceive a baby. He said in a most unconvincing voice, 'Oh—er—of course.' The terrible woman went on. 'I was a *great* friend of your wife's, you know!' "

"They usually say that, too," said Alistair Blunt in a voice of even deeper gloom.

He smiled rather ruefully.

"It always ends the same way! A subscription to something or other. I got off this time with five pounds to a zenana mission or something. Cheap!"

"Had she really known your wife?"

"Well, her being interested in zenana missions made me think that, if so, it would have been in India. We were there about ten years ago. But, of course, she couldn't have been a great friend or I'd have known about it. Probably met her once at a reception."

Jane Olivera said, "I don't believe she'd ever met Aunt Rebecca at all. I think it was just an excuse to speak to you."

Alistair Blunt said tolerantly, "Well, that's quite possible."

Jane said, "I mean, I think it's *queer* the way she tried to scrape an acquaintance with you, Uncle."

Alistair Blunt said with the same tolerance, "She just wanted a subscription."

Poirot said, "She did not try to follow it up in any way?"

Blunt shook his head.

"I never thought of her again. I'd even forgotten her name till Jane spotted it in the paper."

Jane said a little unconvincingly, "Well, *I* thought M.

Poirot ought to be told!"

Poirot said politely, "Thank you, mademoiselle."

He added, "I must not keep you, Mr. Blunt. You are a busy man."

Jane said quickly, "I'll come down with you."

Under his mustaches, Hercule Poirot smiled to himself.

On the ground floor, Jane paused abruptly. She said, "Come in here."

They went into a small room off the hall.

She turned to face him.

"What did you mean on the telephone when you said that you had been expecting me to call you?"

Poirot smiled. He spread out his hands.

"Just that, mademoiselle. I was expecting a call from you—and the call came."

"You mean that you knew I'd ring up about this Sains-bury Seale woman."

Poirot shook his head.

"That was only the pretext. You could have found something else if necessary."

Jane said, "Why the hell *should* I call you up?"

"Why should you deliver this tidbit of information about Miss Sainsbury Seale to *me* instead of giving it to Scotland Yard? That would have been the natural thing to do."

"All right, Mr. Know All, how much exactly *do* you know?"

"I know that you are interested in me since you heard that I paid a visit to the Holborn Palace Hotel the other day."

She went so white that it startled him. He had not believed that that deep tan could change to such a greenish hue.

He went on, quietly and steadily, "You got me to come here today because you wanted to pump me—that is the expression, is it not?—yes, to *pump* me on the subject of

Mr. Howard Raikes."

Jane Olivera said, "Who's he, anyway?"

It was not a very successful parry.

Poirot said, "You do not need to pump me, mademoiselle. I will tell you what I know—or rather what I guessed. That first day that we came here, Inspector Japp and I, you were startled to see us—alarmed. You thought something had happened to your uncle. Why?"

"Well, he's the kind of man things might happen to. He had a bomb by post one day—after the Herjoslovakian Loan. And he gets lots of threatening letters."

Poirot went on.

"Chief Inspector Japp told you that a certain dentist, Mr. Morley, had been shot. You may recollect your answer. You said, '*But that's absurd.*'"

Jane bit her lip. She said, "Did I? That was rather absurd of me, wasn't it?"

"It was a curious remark, mademoiselle. It revealed that you knew of the existence of Mr. Morley, that you had rather expected something to happen—not to happen to him—but possibly to happen in his house."

"You do like telling yourself stories, don't you?"

Poirot paid no attention.

"You had expected—or rather you had feared—that something might happen at Mr. Morley's house. You had feared that something would have happened to your uncle. But if so, *you must know something that we did not know.* I reflected on the people who had been in Mr. Morley's house that day, and I seized at once on the one person who might possibly have a connection with you—which was that young American, Mr. Howard Raikes."

"It's just like a serial, isn't it? What's the next thrilling installment?"

"I went to see Mr. Howard Raikes. He is a dangerous and attractive young man—"

Poirot paused expressively.

Jane said meditatively, "He is, isn't he?" She smiled. "All right! You win! I was scared stiff."

She leaned forward.

"I'm going to tell you things, M. Poirot. You're not the kind one can just string along. I'd rather tell you than have you snooping around finding out. I love that man, Howard Raikes. I'm just crazy about him. My mother brought me over here just to get me away from him. Partly that and partly because she hopes Uncle Alistair might get fond enough of me to leave me his money when he dies."

She went on. "Mother is his niece by marriage. Her mother was Rebecca Arnholt's sister. He's my great-uncle-in-law. Only he hasn't got any near relatives of his own, so mother doesn't see why we shouldn't be his residuary legatees. She cadges off him pretty freely, too.

"You see, I'm being frank with you, M. Poirot. That's the kind of people we are. Actually we've got plenty of money ourselves—an indecent amount according to Howard's ideas—but we're not in Uncle Alistair's class."

She paused. She struck with one hand fiercely on the arm of her chair.

"How can I make you understand? Everything I've been brought up to believe in, Howard abominates and wants to do away with. And sometimes, you know, I feel like he does. I'm fond of Uncle Alistair, but he gets on my nerves sometimes. He's so *stodgy*—so British—so cautious and conservative. I feel sometimes that he and his kind *ought* to be swept away, that they are blocking progress, that without them we'd get things *done!*"

"You are a convert to Mr. Raikes's ideas?"

"I am—and I'm not. Howard is—is wilder than most of his crowd. There are people, you know, who—who agree with Howard up to a point. They would be willing to—to try things—if Uncle Alistair and *his* crowd would agree. But they never will! They just sit back and shake their

heads and say, 'We could never risk that.' And, 'It wouldn't
be sound economically.' And, 'We've got to consider our
responsibility.' And, 'Look at history.' But I think that
one *mustn't* look at history. That's looking back. One
must look *forward* all the time."

Poirot said gently, "It is an attractive vision."

Jane looked at him scornfully.

"You say that, too!"

"Perhaps because I am old. *Their old men have dreams*
—only dreams, you see."

He paused and then asked in a matter-of-fact voice,
"Why did Mr. Howard Raikes make that appointment in
Queen Charlotte Street?"

"Because *I* wanted him to meet Uncle Alistair and I
couldn't see otherwise how to manage it. He'd been so
bitter about Uncle Alister—so full of—of—well, of hate
really, that I felt if he could only see him—see what a nice,
kindly, unassuming person he is—that—that he would feel
differently— I couldn't arrange a meeting here because of
mother—she would have spoiled everything."

Poirot said, "But after having made that arrangement,
you were—afraid."

Her eyes grew wide and dark. She said, "Yes. Because—
because—sometimes Howard gets carried away. He—he—"

Hercule Poirot said, "He wants to take a short cut. To
exterminate—"

Jane Olivera cried, *"Don't!"*

Chapter Four

SEVEN, EIGHT, LAY THEM STRAIGHT

TIME WENT ON. It was over a month since Mr. Morley's death and there was still no news of Miss Sainsbury Seale.

Japp became increasingly wrathful on the subject.

"Dash it all, Poirot, the woman's got to be *somewhere*."

"Indubitably, *mon cher*."

"Either she's dead or alive. If she's dead, where's her body? Say, for instance, she committed suicide—"

"Another suicide?"

"Don't let's get back to that. *You* still say Morley was murdered—*I* say it was suicide."

"You haven't traced the pistol?"

"No, it's a foreign make."

"That is suggestive, is it not?"

"Not in the way you mean. Morley had been abroad. He went on cruises, he and his sister. Everybody in the British Isles goes on cruises. He may have picked it up abroad. Lots of people like a gun when they're abroad. They like to feel life's dangerous."

He paused and said, "Don't sidetrack me. I was saying that *if*—only if, mind you—that blasted woman committed suicide, if she'd drowned herself, for instance, the body would have come ashore by now. If she was murdered, the same thing."

"Not if a weight was attached to her body and it was put into the Thames."

"From a cellar in Limehouse, I suppose! You're talking like a thriller by a lady novelist."

"I know—I know. I blush when I say these things!"

"And she was done to death by an international gang of crooks, I suppose?"

Poirot sighed. He said, "I have been told lately that there really are such things."

"Who told you so?"

"Mr. Reginald Barnes of Castlegardens Road, Ealing."

"Well, he might know," said Japp dubiously. "He dealt with aliens when he was at the Home Office."

"And you do not agree?"

"It isn't my branch—oh, yes, there *are* such things—but they're rather futile as a rule."

There was a momentary silence as Poirot twirled his mustache.

Japp said, "We've got one or two additional bits of information. She came home from India on the same boat as Amberiotis. But she was second class and he was first, so I don't suppose there's anything in that, although one of the waiters at the Savoy thinks she lunched there with him about a week or so before he died."

"So there may have been a connection between them?"

"There may—but I can't feel it's likely. I can't see a missionary lady being mixed up in any funny business."

"Was Amberiotis mixed up in any 'funny business' as you term it?"

"Yes, he was. He was in close touch with some of our Central European friends. Espionage racket."

"You are sure of that?"

"Yes. Oh, he wasn't doing any of the dirty work himself. We wouldn't have been able to touch him. Organizing and receiving reports—that was his lay."

Japp paused and then went on. "But that doesn't help us with the Sainsbury Seale. She wouldn't have been in on that racket."

"She had lived in India, remember. There was a lot of unrest there last year."

"Amberiotis and the excellent Miss Sainsbury Seale—I can't feel they were likely teammates."

"Did you know that Miss Sainsbury Seale was a close

friend of the late Mrs. Alistair Blunt?"

"Who says so? I don't believe it. Not in the same class."

"She said so."

"Who'd she say that to?"

"Mr. Alistair Blunt."

"Oh! That sort of thing. He must be used to that lay. Do you mean that Amberiotis was using her that way? It wouldn't work. Blunt would get rid of her with a subscription. He wouldn't ask her down for a week-end or anything of that kind. He's not so unsophisticated as that."

This was so palpably true that Poirot could only agree. After a minute or two, Japp went on with his summing up of the Sainsbury Seale situation.

"I suppose her body might have been lowered into a tank of acid by a mad scientist—that's another solution they're very fond of in books! But take my word for it, these things are all my eye and Betty Martin. If the woman *is* dead, her body has just been quietly buried somewhere."

"But where?"

"Exactly. She disappeared in London. Nobody's got a garden there—not a proper one. A lonely chicken farm, that's what we want!"

A garden? Poirot's mind flashed suddenly to that neat prim garden at Ealing with its formal beds. How fantastic if a dead woman should be buried *there!*

He told himself not to be absurd.

"And if she *isn't* dead," went on Japp, "where is she? Over a month now, description published in the *Press*, circulated all over England—"

"And nobody has seen her?"

"Oh, yes, practically *everybody* has seen her! You've no idea how many middle-aged, faded-looking women wearing olive-green cardigan suits there are. She's been seen on Yorkshire moors and in Liverpool hotels, in guest houses in Devon and on the beach at Ramsgate! My men

have spent their time patiently investigating all these reports—and one and all they've led nowhere, except to
getting us in wrong with a number of perfectly respectable
middle-aged ladies."

Poirot clicked his tongue sympathetically.

"And yet," went on Japp, "she's a real person all right.
I mean sometimes you come across a dummy, so to speak—
someone who just comes to a place and poses as a Miss
Spinks—when all the time there *isn't* a Miss Spinks. But
this woman's *genuine*—she's got a past, a background! We
know all about her from her childhood upward. She's led
a perfectly normal reasonable life—and suddenly, hey,
presto!—vanish!"

"There must be a reason," said Poirot.

"She didn't shoot Morley, if that's what you mean.
Amberiotis saw him alive after she left—and we've checked
up on her movements after she left Queen Charlotte
Street that morning."

Poirot said impatiently, "I am not suggesting for a moment that she shot Morley. Of course she did not. But all
the same—"

Japp said, "If you are right about Morley, then it's far
more likely that he told her something which, although
she doesn't suspect it, gives a clue to his murderer. In that
case, she *might* have been deliberately put out of the way."

Poirot said, "All this involves an organization, some
big concern quite out of proportion to the death of a quiet
dentist in Queen Charlotte Street."

"Don't you believe everything Reginald Barnes tells
you! He's a funny old bird—got spies and Communists on
the brain."

Japp got up and Poirot said, "Let me know if you have
news."

When Japp had gone out, Poirot sat frowning down at
the table in front of him.

He had definitely the feeling of waiting for something.

What was it?

He remembered how he had sat before, jotting down various unrelated facts and a series of names. A bird had flown past the window with a twig in its mouth.

He, too, had been collecting twigs. *Five, six, pick up sticks—*

He had the sticks—quite a number of them now. They were all there, neatly pigeonholed in his orderly mind—but he had not as yet attempted to set them in order. That was the next step—*lay them straight.*

What was holding him up? He knew the answer. He was waiting for something.

Something inevitable, foreordained, the next link in the chain. When it came—then—*then* he could go on.

It was late evening a week later when the summons came.

Japp's voice was brusque over the telephone.

"That you, Poirot? *We've found her.* You'd better come round. King Leopold Mansions. Battersea Park. Number forty-five."

A quarter of an hour later a taxi deposited Poirot outside King Leopold Mansions.

It was a big block of mansion flats looking out over Battersea Park. Number 45 was on the second floor. Japp himself opened the door.

His face was set in grim lines.

"Come in," he said. "It's not particularly pleasant, but I expect you'll want to see for yourself."

Poirot said—but it was hardly a question, "Dead?"

"What you might describe as very dead!"

Poirot cocked his head at a familiar sound coming from a door on his right.

"That's the porter," said Japp, "being sick in the scullery sink! I had to get him up here to see if he could identify her."

He led the way down the passage and Poirot followed him. His nose wrinkled.

"Not nice," said Japp. "But what can you expect? She's been dead well over a month."

The room they went into was a small lumber and box room. In the middle of it was a big metal chest of the kind used for storing furs. The lid was open.

Poirot stepped forward and looked inside.

He saw the foot first, with the shabby shoe on it and the ornate buckle. His first sight of Miss Sainsbury Seale had been, he remembered, a shoe buckle.

His gaze traveled up, over the green wool coat and skirt till it reached the head.

He made an inarticulate noise.

"I know," said Japp. "It's pretty horrible."

The face had been battered out of all recognizable shape. Add to that the natural processes of decomposition, and it was no wonder that both men looked a shade pea-green as they turned away.

"Oh, well," said Japp. "It's all in the day's work—our day's work. No doubt about it, ours is a lousy job sometimes. There's a spot of brandy in the other room. You'd better have some."

The living-room was smartly furnished in an up-to-date style—a good deal of chromium and some large, square-looking easy chairs upholstered in a pale fawn geometric fabric.

Poirot found the decanter and helped himself to some brandy. As he finished drinking, he said, "It was not pretty, that! Now tell me, my friend, all about it."

Japp said, "This flat belongs to a Mrs. Albert Chapman. Mrs. Chapman is, I gather, a well-upholstered smart blonde of forty-odd. Pays her bills, fond of an occasional game of bridge with her neighbors, but keeps to herself more or less. No children. Mr. Chapman is a commercial traveler.

"Sainsbury Seale came here on the evening of our interview with her. About seven-fifteen. So she probably came straight here from the Glengowrie Court. She'd been here once before, so the porter says. You see, all perfectly clear and aboveboard—nice friendly call. The porter took Miss Sainsbury Seale up in the elevator to this flat. The last he saw of her she was standing on the mat pressing the bell."

Poirot commented, "He has taken his time to remember this!"

"He's had gastric trouble, it seems, been away in hospital while another man took on temporarily for him. It wasn't until about a week ago that he happened to notice in an old paper the description of a 'wanted woman' and he said to his wife, 'Sounds quite like that old cup of tea who came to see Mrs. Chapman on the second floor. *She* had on a green wool dress and buckles on her shoes.' And after about another hour he registered again—'Believe she had a name, too, something like that. Blimey, it *was*— Miss Something or other Seale.'

"After that," continued Japp, "it took him about four days to overcome his natural distrust of getting mixed up with the police and come along with his information.

"We didn't really think it would lead to anything. You've no idea of how many of these false alarms we've had. However, I sent Sergeant Beddoes along—he's a bright young fellow. A bit too much of this high class education but he can't help that. It's fashionable now.

"Well, Beddoes got a hunch at once that we were on to something at last. For one thing, this Mrs. Chapman hadn't been seen about for over a month. She'd gone away without leaving any address. That was a bit odd. In fact, everything he could learn about Mr. and Mrs. Chapman seemed odd.

"He found out the porter hadn't seen Miss Sainsbury Seale leave again. That in itself wasn't unusual. She might easily have come down the stairs and gone out without his seeing her. But then the porter told him that Mrs. Chapman had gone away rather suddenly. There was just a big printed notice outside the door the next morning: 'No milk tell Nellie I am called away.'

"Nellie was the daily maid who did for her. Mrs. Chapman had gone away suddenly once or twice before, so the girl didn't think it odd, but what *was* odd was the fact that she hadn't rung for the porter to take her luggage down or get her a taxi.

"Anyway, Beddoes decided to get into the flat. We got a search warrant and a pass key from the manager. Found nothing of interest except in the bathroom. There had been some hasty clearing up done there. There was a trace of blood on the linoleum—in the corners where it had been missed when the floor was washed over. After that, it was just a question of finding the body. Mrs. Chapman couldn't have left with any luggage with her or the porter would have known. Therefore the body *must* still be in the flat. We soon spotted that fur chest—airtight, you know—just the place. Keys were in the dressing-table drawer.

"We opened it up—and there was the missing lady! *Mistletoe Bough* up to date."

Poirot asked, "What about Mrs. Chapman?"

"What indeed? 'Who is Sylvia'—her name's Sylvia, by the way—'what is she?' One thing is certain. Sylvia, or Sylvia's friends, murdered the lady and put her in the box."

Poirot nodded.

He asked, "But why was her face battered in? It is not nice, that."

"I'll say it isn't nice! As to *why*—well, one can only guess. Sheer vindictiveness, perhaps. Or it may have been with the idea of concealing the woman's identity."

Poirot frowned. He said, "But it did *not* conceal her

identity."

"No, because not only had we got a pretty good description of what Mabelle Sainsbury Seale was wearing when she disappeared, but her handbag had been stuffed into the fur box, too, and inside the handbag there was actually an old letter addressed to her at her hotel in Russell Square."

Poirot sat up. He said, "But that—that does not make the common sense!"

"It certainly doesn't. I suppose it was a slip."

"Yes—perhaps—a slip. But—"

He got up.

"You have been over the flat?"

"Pretty well. There's nothing illuminating."

"I should like to see Mrs. Chapman's bedroom."

"Come along then."

The bedroom showed no signs of a hasty departure. It was neat and tidy. The bed had not been slept in, but was turned down ready for the night. There was a thick coating of dust everywhere.

Japp said, "No fingerprints, so far as we can see. There are some on the kitchen things, but I expect they'll turn out to be the maid's."

"That means that the whole place was dusted very carefully after the murder?"

"Yes."

Poirot's eyes swept slowly round the room. Like the sitting-room it was furnished in the modern style—and furnished, so he thought, by someone with a moderate income. The articles in it were expensive but not ultra-expensive. They were showy but not first class. The color scheme was rose pink. He looked into the built-in wardrobe and handled the clothes—smart clothes but again not of first-class quality. His eyes fell to the shoes—they were largely of the sandal variety popular at the moment; some had exaggerated cork soles. He balanced one in his hand, registered the fact that Mrs. Chapman had taken a size five in shoes and put it down again. In another cupboard he found a pile of furs, shoved in in a heap.

Japp said, "Came out of the fur chest."

Poirot nodded.

He was handling a grey squirrel coat. He remarked appreciatively, "First-class skins."

He went on into the bathroom.

There was a lavish display of cosmetics. Poirot looked at them with interest. Powder, rouge, vanishing cream, skin food, two bottles of hair application.

Japp said, "Not one of our natural platinum blondes, I gather."

Poirot murmured, "At forty, *mon ami,* the hair of most women has begun to go gray but Mrs. Chapman was not one to yield to nature."

"She's probably gone henna red by now for a change."

"I wonder?"

Japp said, "There's something worrying you, Poirot. What is it?"

Poirot said, "But yes, I am worried. I am very seriously worried. There is here, you see, for me an insoluble problem."

Resolutely he went once more into the box room—

He took hold of the shoe on the dead woman's foot. It resisted and came off with difficulty.

He examined the buckle. It had been clumsily sewed on by hand.

Hercule Poirot sighed.

He said, "It is that I am dreaming!"

Japp said curiously, "What are you trying to do—make the thing more difficult?"

"Exactly that."

Japp said, "One patent-leather shoe, complete with buckle. What's wrong with that?"

Hercule Poirot said: "Nothing—absolutely nothing. But all the same—I do not understand."

Mrs. Merton of 82 King Leopold Mansions had been designated by the porter as Mrs. Chapman's closest friend in the Mansions.

It was, therefore, to 82 that Japp and Poirot betook themselves next.

Mrs. Merton was a loquacious lady, with snapping black eyes, and an elaborate coiffure.

It needed no pressure to make her talk. She was only too ready to rise to a dramatic situation.

"Sylvia Chapman—well, of course, I don't know her really well—not intimately, so to speak. We had a few bridge evenings occasionally and we went to the pictures together, and, of course, shopping sometimes. But, oh, do tell me—she isn't *dead*, is she?"

Japp reassured her.

"Well, I'm sure I'm thankful to hear it! But the postman just now was all agog about a body having been found in one of the flats—but then one really can't believe half one hears, can one? I *never* do."

Japp asked a further question.

"No, I haven't heard anything of Mrs. Chapman—not since she went away. She must have gone away rather suddenly, because we had spoken about going to see the new Ginger Rogers and Fred Astaire the following week, and she said nothing about going away *then*."

Mrs. Merton had never heard a Miss Sainsbury Seale mentioned. Mrs. Chapman had never spoken of anyone of that name.

"And yet, you know, the name *is* familiar to me, distinctly familiar. I seem to have seen it somewhere quite *lately*."

Japp said dryly, "It's been in all the papers for some weeks—"

"Of course—some missing person, wasn't it? And you thought Mrs. Chapman might have known her? No, I'm sure I've never heard Sylvia mention *that* name."

"Can you tell me anything about Mr. Chapman, Mrs. Merton?"

A rather curious expression came over Mrs. Merton's face. She said, "He was a commercial traveler, I believe, so Mrs. Chapman told me. He traveled abroad for his firm—armaments, I believe. He went all over Europe."

"Did you ever meet him?"

"No, never. He was at home so seldom, and when he was at home, he and Mrs. Chapman didn't want to bother with outsiders. Very naturally."

"Do you know if Mrs. Chapman had any near relations or friends?"

"I don't know about friends. I don't think she had any near relations. She never spoke of any."

"Was she ever in India?"

"Not that I know of."

Mrs. Merton paused, and then broke out, "But please tell me—why are you asking all these questions? I quite understand that you come from Scotland Yard and all that, but there must be some special reason?"

"Well, Mrs. Merton, you are bound to know some time. As a matter of fact, a dead body *has* been found in Mrs. Chapman's flat."

"Oh!" Mrs. Merton looked for a moment like the dog whose eyes were as big as saucers.

"A dead body! It wasn't Mr. Chapman, was it? Or perhaps some foreigner?"

Japp said, "It wasn't a man at all—it was a woman."

"A woman?" Mrs. Merton seemed even more surprised.

Poirot said gently, "Why should you think it was a man?"

"Oh, I don't know. It seemed more likely somehow."

"But why? Was it because Mrs. Chapman was in the

habit of receiving gentlemen visitors?"

"Oh, no—oh, no, indeed." Mrs. Merton was indignant. "I never meant anything of *that* kind. Sylvia Chapman wasn't in the least *that* kind of a woman—not at all! It was just that, with Mr. Chapman—I mean—"

She came to a stop.

Poirot said, "I think, madame, that you know a little more than you have told us."

Mrs. Merton said uncertainly, "I don't know, I'm sure— *what* I ought to do! I mean, I don't exactly want to betray a confidence and, of course, I never have repeated what Sylvia told me—except just to one or two intimates whom I knew were really *safe*—"

Mrs. Merton paused to draw breath. Japp said, "What *did* Mrs. Chapman tell you?"

Mrs. Merton leaned forward and lowered her voice.

"It just—slipped out, as it were, one day. When we were seeing a film—about the secret service and Mrs. Chapman said you could see that whoever had written it didn't know much about their subject, and then it came out— only she swore me to secrecy. Mr. Chapman was in the secret service, I mean. That was the real reason he had to go abroad so much. The armament firm was only a blind. And it was terribly worrying for Mrs. Chapman because she couldn't write to him or get letters from him while he was away. And, of course, it was terribly *dangerous!*"

As they went down the stairs again to Number 42, Japp ejaculated with feeling, "Shades of Phillips Oppenheim, Valentine Williams, and William le Quex! I think I'm going mad!"

That smart young man, Sergeant Beddoes, was awaiting them.

He said respectfully, "Haven't been able to get anything helpful from the maid, sir. Mrs. Chapman changed maids pretty often, it seems. This one had only worked for her a month or two. She says Mrs. Chapman was a nice lady, fond of the radio, and pleasant spoken. Girl was of opinion the husband was a gay deceiver but that Mrs. Chapman didn't suspect it. She got letters from abroad sometimes, some from Germany, two from America, one from Italy, and one from Russia. The girl's young man collects stamps, and Mrs. Chapman used to give them to her off the letters."

"Anything among Mrs. Chapman's papers?"

"Absolutely nothing, sir. She didn't keep much. A few bills and receipted accounts—all local. Some old theater programs, one or two cookery recipes cut out of the papers, and a pamphlet about zenana missions."

"And we can guess who brought *that* here. She doesn't sound like a murderess, does she? And yet that's what it seems to be. She's bound to be an accomplice anyway. No strange men seen about that evening?"

"The porter doesn't remember any—but then I don't suppose he would by now, and anyway it's a big block of flats—people always going in and out. He can only fix the date of Miss Sainsbury Seale's visit because he was taken off to the hospital the next day and was actually feeling rather bad that evening."

"Anybody in the other flats hear anything out of the way?"

The younger man shook his head.

"I've inquired at the flat above this and the one below. Nobody can remember hearing anything unusual. Both of them had their radios on, I gather."

The divisional surgeon came out of the bathroom where he had been washing his hands.

"Most unsavory corpse," he said cheerfully. "Send her along when you're ready and I'll get down to brass tacks."

"No idea of the cause of death, doctor?"

"Impossible to say until I've done the autopsy. Those face injuries were definitely inflicted after death, I should say. But I shall know better when I've got her at the mortuary. Middle-aged woman, quite healthy—gray hair at the roots but tinted blond. There may be distinguishing marks on the body— If there aren't, it may be a job to identify her— Oh, you know who she is? That's splendid. What? Missing woman there's been all the fuss about? Well, you know, I never read the papers. Just do the crosswords."

Japp said bitterly, "And that's publicity for you!" as the doctor went out.

Poirot was hovering over the desk. He picked up a small brown address book.

The indefatigable Beddoes said, "Nothing of special interest there—mostly hairdressers, dressmakers, etc. I've noted down any private names and addresses."

Poirot opened the book at the letter D.

He read: *Dr. Davis, 17 Prince Albert Road; Drake and Pomponetti, Fishmongers.* And below it: *Dentist, Mr. Morley, 58 Queen Charlotte Street.*

There was a green light in Poirot's eyes. He said, "There will be no difficulty, I imagine, in positively identifying the body."

Japp looked at him curiously. He said, "Surely—you don't imagine?"

Poirot said with vehemence, "I want to be *sure.*"

Miss Morley had moved to the country. She was living in a small country cottage near Hertford.

The grenadier greeted Poirot amicably. Since her brother's death her face had perhaps grown slightly grimmer, her carriage more upright, her general attitude toward life more unyielding. She resented bitterly the slur cast upon her brother's professional name by the findings of the inquest.

Poirot, she had reason to believe, shared her view that the verdict of the coroner's court was untrue. Hence the grenadier unbent a little.

She answered his questions readily enough and with competence. All Mr. Morley's professional papers had been carefully filed by Miss Nevill and had been handed over by her to Mr. Morley's successor. Some of the patients had transferred themselves to Mr. Reilly, others had accepted the new partner, others again had gone to other dentists elsewhere.

Miss Morley, after she had given what information she could, said, "So you have found that woman who was Henry's patient—Miss Sainsbury Seale—and *she* was murdered, *too*."

The "too" was a little defiant. She stressed the word.

Poirot said, "Your brother never mentioned Miss Sainsbury Seale particularly to you?"

"No, I don't remember his doing so. He would tell me if he had had a particularly trying patient, or if one of his patients had said something amusing he would pass it on to me, but we didn't usually talk much about his work. He was glad to forget it when the day was over. He was very tired sometimes."

"Do you remember hearing of a Mrs. Chapman among your brother's patients?"

"Chapman? No, I don't think so. Miss Nevill is really the person to help you over all this."

"I am anxious to get in touch with her. Where is she now?"

"She has taken a post with a dentist in Ramsgate, I believe."

"She has not married that young man Frank Carter yet?"

"No. I rather hope that will never come off. I don't like that young man, M. Poirot. I really don't. There is something wrong about him. I still feel that he hasn't really any proper moral sense."

Poirot said, "Do you think it is possible that *he* could

have shot your brother?"

Miss Morley said slowly, "I do feel perhaps that he would be *capable* of it—he has a very uncontrollable temper. But I don't really see that he had any motive—nor opportunity for that matter. You see, it wasn't as though Henry had succeeded in persuading Gladys to give him up. She was sticking to him in the most faithful way."

"Could he have been bribed do you think?"

"Bribed? To kill my brother? What an extraordinary idea!"

A nice-looking dark-haired girl brought in the tea at this moment. As she closed the door behind her again, Poirot said, "That girl was with you in London, was she not?"

"Agnes? Yes, she was house-parlormaid. I let the cook go—she didn't want to come to the country anyway—and Agnes does everything for me. She is turning into quite a nice little cook."

Poirot nodded.

He knew very accurately the domestic arrangements of 58 Queen Charlotte Street. They had been thoroughly gone into at the time of the tragedy. Mr. Morley and his sister had occupied the two top floors of the house as a maisonette. The basement had been shut up altogether, except for a narrow passage leading from the area to the back yard where a wire cage ran up to the top floor with the tradesmen's deliveries and where a speaking-tube was installed. Therefore the only entrance to the house was by the front door which it was Alfred's business to answer. This had enabled the police to be sure that no outsider could have entered the house on that particular morning.

Both cook and house-parlormaid had been with the Morleys for some years and bore good characters. So, although it was theoretically possible that one or other of them *might* have crept down to the second floor and shot her master, the possibility had never been taken seriously into account. Neither of the two had appeared unduly flustered or upset at being questioned, and there certainly seemed no possible reason for connecting either of them with his death.

Nevertheless, as Agnes handed Poirot his hat and stick on leaving, she asked him with an unusually nervous abruptness, "Does—does anyone know anything more about the master's death, sir?"

Poirot turned to look at her. He said, "Nothing fresh has come to light."

"They're still quite sure as he *did* shoot himself because he'd made a mistake with that drug?"

"Yes. Why do you ask?"

Agnes pleated her apron. Her face was averted. She said rather indistinctly, "The—the mistress doesn't think so."

"And you agree with her, perhaps?"

"Me? Oh, I don't know nothing, sir. I only—I only wanted to be *sure*."

Hercule Poirot said in his most gentle voice, "It would be a relief to you to feel beyond any possible doubt that it *was* suicide?"

"Oh, yes, sir," Agnes agreed quickly, "it would indeed."

"For a special reason, perhaps?"

Her startled eyes met his. She shrank back a little.

"I—I don't know anything about it, sir. I only just asked."

"But *why* did she ask?" Hercule Poirot demanded of himself as he walked down the path to the gate.

He felt sure that there was an answer to that question. But as yet he could not guess what it was.

All the same, he felt a step nearer.

When Poirot returned to his flat he was surprised to find an unexpected visitor awaiting him.

A bald head was visible above the back of a chair, and the small neat figure of Mr. Barnes rose to his feet.

With eyes that twinkled as usual, he made a dry little apology. He had come, he explained, to return M. Hercule Poirot's visit.

Poirot professed himself delighted to see Mr. Barnes. George was instructed to bring some coffee unless his visitor preferred tea or whisky and soda?

"Coffee will be admirable," said Mr. Barnes. "I imagine that your manservant prepares it well. Most English servants do not."

Presently, after a few interchanges of polite remarks, Mr. Barnes gave a little cough and said, "I will be frank with you, M. Poirot. It was sheer curiosity that brought me here. You, I imagined, would be well posted in all the details of this rather curious case. I see by the papers that the missing Miss Sainsbury Seale has been found, that an inquest was held and adjourned for further evidence. Cause of death was stated to have been an overdose of medinal."

"That is quite correct," said Poirot.

There was a pause and then Poirot said, "Have you ever heard of Albert Chapman, Mr. Barnes?"

"Ah, the husband of the lady in whose flat Miss Sainsbury Seale came to die? Rather an elusive person, it would seem."

"But hardly non-existent?"

"Oh, no," said Mr. Barnes. "He exists. Oh, yes, he exists —or *did* exist. I had heard he was dead. But you can't trust these rumors."

"Who was he, Mr. Barnes?"

"I don't suppose they'll say at the inquest. Not if they can help it. They'll trot out the armaments firm traveler story."

"He *was* in the secret service, then?"

"Of course he was. But he had no business to tell his wife so—no business at all. In fact, he ought not to have continued in the service after his marriage. It isn't usually done—not, that is, when you're one of the really hush-hush people."

"And Albert Chapman was?"

"Yes. Q.X.912. That's what he was known as. Using a name is most irregular. Oh, I don't mean that Q.X.912 was specially important—or anything of that kind. But he was useful because he was an insignificant sort of chap—the kind whose face isn't easily remembered. He was used a lot as a messenger up and down Europe. You know the sort of thing. One dignified letter sent via our ambassador in Ruritania—one unofficial ditto containing the dirt per Q.X.912—that is to say, Mr. Albert Chapman."

"Then he knew a lot of useful information?"

"Probably didn't know a thing," said Mr. Barnes cheerfully. "His job was just hopping in and out of trains and boats and airplanes and having the right story to explain *why* he was going *where* he was going!"

"And you heard he was dead?"

"That's what I heard," said Mr. Barnes. "But you can't believe all you hear. I never do."

Looking at Mr. Barnes intently, Poirot asked, "What do you think has happened to his wife?"

"I can't imagine," said Mr. Barnes. He looked, wide-eyed, at Poirot. "Can you?"

Poirot said, "I had an idea—" He stopped.

He said slowly, "It is very confusing."

Mr. Barnes murmured sympathetically, "Anything worrying you in particular?"

Hercule Poirot said slowly, "Yes. The evidence of my own eyes."

Japp came into Poirot's sitting-room and slammed down his bowler hat with such force that the table rocked.

He said, "What the devil made you think of it?"

"My good Japp, I do not know what you are talking about."

Japp said slowly and forcefully, "What gave you the idea that body wasn't Miss Sainsbury Seale's body?"

Poirot looked worried. He said, "It was the face that worried me. Why smash up a dead woman's face?"

Japp said, "My word, I hope old Morley's somewhere where he can know about it. It's just possible, you know, that he was put out of the way on purpose—so that he couldn't give evidence."

"It would certainly be better if he could have given evidence himself."

"Leatheran will be all right. Morley's successor. He's a thoroughly capable man with a good manner and the evidence is unmistakable."

The evening papers came out with a sensation the next day. The dead body found in the Battersea flat, believed to be that of Miss Sainsbury Seale, was positively identified as that of Mrs. Albert Chapman.

Mr. Leatheran, of 58 Queen Charlotte Street, unhesitatingly pronounced it to be Mrs. Chapman on the evidence of the teeth and jaw, full particulars of which were recorded in the late Mr. Morley's professional chart.

Miss Sainsbury Seale's clothes had been found on the body and Miss Sainsbury Seale's handbag with the body—but where was Miss Sainsbury Seale herself?

Chapter Five

NINE, TEN, A GOOD FAT HEN

AS THEY CAME AWAY FROM THE INQUEST Japp said jubilantly to Poirot, "A smart piece of work, that. Gave 'em a sensation!"

Poirot nodded.

"You tumbled to it first," said Japp, "but, you know, I wasn't happy about that body myself. After all, you don't go smashing a dead person's face and head about for nothing. It's messy, unpleasant work, and it was pretty plain there must be *some* reason for it. There's only one reason there could be—to confuse the identity." He added generously, "But I shouldn't have tumbled so quickly to the fact that it actually was the other woman."

Poirot said with a smile, "And yet, my friend, the actual descriptions of the women were not unlike as regards fundamentals. Mrs. Chapman was a smart, good-looking woman, well made up and fashionably turned out. Miss Sainsbury Seale was dowdy and innocent of lipstick or rouge. But the essentials were the same. Both were women of forty-odd. Both were roughly about the same height and build. Both had hair turning gray which they touched up to make it appear golden."

"Yes, of course, when you put it like *that*. One thing we've got to admit—the fair Mabelle put it over on both of us, good and proper. I'd have sworn she was the genuine article."

"But, my friend, she *was* the genuine article. We know all about her past life."

"We didn't know she was capable of murder—and that's what it looks like now. Sylvia didn't murder Mabelle. Mabelle murdered Sylvia."

Hercule Poirot shook his head in a worried fashion. He

still found it difficult to reconcile Mabelle Sainsbury Seale with murder. Yet in his ears he heard the small, ironic voice of Mr. Barnes, "Look among the respectable people—"

Mabelle Sainsbury Seale had been eminently respectable.

Japp said with emphasis, "I'm going to get to the bottom of this case, Poirot. That woman isn't going to put it over on me."

The following day Japp rang up. His voice held a curious note. He said, "Poirot, do you want to hear a piece of news? It's Na Poo, my lad. Na Poo!"

"*Pardon?* The line is perhaps not very clear. I did not quite catch—"

"It's off, my boy. O.F.F. Call it a day! Sit down and twiddle our thumbs!"

There was no mistaking the bitterness now. Poirot was startled. "What is off?"

"The whole ruddy blinking thing! The hue and cry! The publicity! The whole bag of tricks!"

"But I still do not understand."

"Well, listen. Listen carefully, because I can't mention names very well. You know our inquiry? You know we're combing the country for a performing fish?"

"Yes, yes, perfectly. I comprehend now."

"Well, that's been called *off*. Hushed up—kept mum. *Now* do you understand?"

"Yes, yes. But *why?*"

"Orders from the ruddy Foreign Office."

"Is not that very extraordinary?"

"Well, it does happen now and again."

"Why should they be so forbearing to Miss—to the performing fish?"

"They're not. They don't care tuppence about her. It's the publicity—if she's brought to trial too much might come out about Mrs. A.C. The corpse. That's the hush-hush side! I can only suppose that the ruddy husband—Mr. A.C.— Get me?"

"Yes, yes."

"That he's somewhere abroad in a ticklish spot and they don't want to queer his pitch."

"Tchah!"

"What did you say?"

"I made, *mon ami,* an exclamation of annoyance!"

"Oh! That was it. I thought you'd caught cold. Annoyance is right! I could use a stronger word. Letting that dame get away with it makes me see red."

Poirot said very softly, "She will not get away with it."

"Our hands are tied, I tell you!"

"Yours may be—*mine* are not!"

"Good old Poirot! Then you *are* going on with it?"

"*Mais oui*—to the death."

"Well, don't let it be your death, old boy! If this business goes on as it has begun someone will probably send you a poisoned tarantula by post!"

As he replaced the receiver, Poirot said to himself, "Now why did I use that melodramatic phrase—'to the death'? *Vraiment,* it is absurd!"

The letter came by the evening post. It was typewritten except for the signature:

Dear M. Poirot:

I should be greatly obliged if you would call upon me some time tomorrow. I may have a commission for you. I suggest twelve-thirty, at my house in Chelsea. If this is inconvenient to you, perhaps you would telephone and arrange some other time with my secretary? I apologize for giving you such short notice.

Yours sincerely,

Alistair Blunt.

Poirot smoothed out the letter and read it a second time. At that moment the telephone rang.

Hercule Poirot occasionally indulged in the fancy that he knew by the ring of his telephone bell what kind of message was impending.

On this occasion he was at once quite sure that the call was significant. It was not a wrong number—not one of his friends.

He got up and took down the receiver. He said in his polite, foreign voice, *"Allô?"*

An impersonal voice said, "What number are you, please?"

"This is Whitehall 7272."

There was a pause, a click, and then a voice spoke. It was a woman's voice.

"M. Poirot?"

"Yes."

"M. Hercule Poirot?"

"Yes."

"M. Poirot, you have either already received—or will shortly receive—a letter."

"Who is speaking?"

"It is not necessary that you should know."

"Very well. I have received, madame, eight letters and three bills by the evening post."

"Then you know which letter I mean. You will be wise, M. Poirot, to refuse the commission you have been offered."

"That, madame, is a matter I shall decide myself."

The voice said coldly, "I am warning you, M. Poirot. Your interference will no longer be tolerated. *Keep out of this business.*"

"And if I do not keep out of it?"

"Then we shall take steps to see that your interference is no longer to be feared."

"That is a threat, madame!"

"We are only asking you to be sensible. It is for your own good."

"You are very magnanimous!"

"You cannot alter the course of events and what has been arranged. *So keep out of what doesn't concern you!* Do you understand?"

"Oh, yes, I understand. But I consider that Mr. Morley's death *is* my concern."

The woman's voice said sharply, "Morley's death was only an incident. He interfered with our plans."

"He was a human being, madame, and he died before his time."

"He was of no importance."

Poirot's voice was dangerous as he said very quietly, "There you are wrong."

"It was his own fault. He refused to be sensible."

"I, too, refuse to be sensible."

"Then you are a fool."

There was a click at the other end as the receiver was replaced.

Poirot said, *"Allô?"* then put down his receiver in turn. He did not trouble to ask the exchange to trace the number. He was fairly sure that the call had been put through from a public telephone box.

What intrigued and puzzled him was the fact that he thought he had heard the voice somewhere before. He racked his brains, trying to bring the elusive memory back. Could it be the voice of Miss Sainsbury Seale?

As he remembered it, Mabelle Sainsbury Seale's voice had been high-pitched and somewhat affected, with rather over-emphasized diction. This voice was not at all like that, and yet—perhaps it might be Miss Sainsbury Seale with her voice disguised. After all, she had been an actress in her time. She could alter her voice, probably, easily enough. In actual timbre, the voice was not unlike what he remembered.

But he was not satisfied with that explanation. No, it was some other person that the voice brought back to him. It was not a voice he knew well—but he was still quite sure that he had heard it once, if not twice, before.

Why, he wondered, bother to ring up and threaten him? Could these people actually believe that threats would deter him? Apparently they did. It was poor psychology!

There was some sensational news in the morning papers. The Prime Minister had been shot at when leaving 10 Downing Street with a friend yesterday evening. Fortunately the bullet had gone wide. The man, an Indian, had been taken into custody.

After reading this, Poirot took a taxi to Scotland Yard where he was shown up to Japp's room. The latter greeted him heartily.

"Ah, so the news has brought you along. Have any of the papers mentioned who 'the friend' was with the P.M.?"

"No, who was it?"

"Alistair Blunt."

"Really?"

"And," went on Japp, "we've every reason to believe that the bullet was meant for Blunt and not for the P.M. That is, unless the man was an even more thundering bad shot than he is already!"

"Who did it?"

"Some crazy Hindu student. Half-baked, as usual. But he was put up to it. It wasn't all his own idea."

Japp added, "Quite a sound bit of work getting him. There's usually a small group of people, you know, watching Number Ten. When the shot was fired, a young American grabbed hold of a little man with a beard. Held on to him like grim death and yelled to the police that he'd got the man. Meanwhile the Indian was quietly hooking it—but one of our people nabbed him all right."

"Who was the American?" asked Poirot curiously.

"Young fellow by the name of Raikes. Why—" he stopped short, staring at Poirot. "What's the matter?"

Poirot said, "Howard Raikes, staying at the Holborn Palace Hotel."

"That's right. Who—why, of course! I thought the name seemed familiar. He's the patient who ran away that morning when Morley shot himself."

He paused. He said slowly, "Rum—how that old business keeps cropping up. You've still got your ideas about it, haven't you, Poirot?"

Hercule Poirot replied gravely, "Yes. I still have my ideas."

At the Gothic House, Poirot was received by a secretary, a tall, limp young man with an accomplished social manner.

He was pleasantly apologetic.

"I am so sorry, M. Poirot—and so is Mr. Blunt. He has been called to Downing Street. The result of this—er—incident last night. I rang your flat, but unfortunately you had already left."

The young man went on rapidly, "Mr. Blunt commissioned me to ask you if it would be possible for you to spend the week-end with him at his house in Kent. Exsham, you know. If so, he would call for you in the car tomorrow evening."

Poirot hesitated.

The young man said persuasively, "Mr. Blunt is really most anxious to see you."

Hercule Poirot bowed his head.

He said, "Thank you. I accept."

"Oh, that's splendid. Mr. Blunt will be delighted. If he calls for you about a quarter to six, will that— Oh, good morning, Mrs. Olivera—"

Jane Olivera's mother had just entered. She was very smartly dressed, with a hat clinging to an eyebrow in the midst of a very *soignée* coiffure.

"Oh! Mr. Selby, did Mr. Blunt give you any instructions about those garden chairs? I meant to talk to him about them last night, because I knew we'd be going down this week-end and—"

Mrs. Olivera took in Poirot and paused.

"Do you know Mrs. Olivera, M. Poirot?"

"I have already had the pleasure of meeting madame." Poirot bowed.

Mrs. Olivera said vaguely, "Oh? How do you do? Of course, Mr. Selby, I know that Alistair is a very busy man and that these small domestic matters mayn't seem to him important—"

"It's quite all right, Mrs. Olivera," said the efficient Mr. Selby. "He told me about it and I rang up Messrs. Deevers about them."

"Well, now, that's a real load off my mind. Now, Mr. Selby, can you tell me—"

Mrs. Olivera clacked on. She was, thought Poirot, rather like a hen. A big, fat hen! Mrs. Olivera, still clacking, moved majestically after her bust toward the door.

"—and if you're quite sure that there will only be ourselves this week-end—"

Mr. Selby coughed.

"Er—M. Poirot is also coming down for the week-end."

Mrs. Olivera stopped. She turned round and surveyed Poirot with visible distaste.

"Is that really so?"

"Mr. Blunt has been kind enough to invite me," said Poirot.

"Well, I wonder—why, if that isn't *queer* of Alistair. You'll excuse me, M. Poirot, but Mr. Blunt particularly told me that he wanted a quiet, *family* week-end!"

Selby said firmly, "Mr. Blunt is particularly anxious

that M. Poirot should come."

"Oh, really? He didn't mention it to *me*."

The door opened. Jane stood there. She said impatiently, "Mother, aren't you coming? Our lunch appointment is at one-fifteen!"

"I'm coming, Jane. Don't be impatient."

"Well, get a move on, for goodness' sake— Hullo, M. Poirot."

She was suddenly very still—her petulance frozen, her eyes more wary.

Mrs. Olivera said in a cold voice, "M. Poirot is coming down to Exsham for the week-end."

"Oh—I see."

Jane Olivera stood back to let her mother pass her. On the point of following her, she whirled back again.

"M. Poirot!"

Her voice was imperious.

Poirot crossed the room to her.

She said in a low voice, "You're coming down to Exsham? Why?"

Poirot shrugged his shoulders. He said, "It is a kind thought of your uncle's."

Jane said, "But he can't know— He can't— When did he ask you? Oh, there's no need—"

"Jane!"

Her mother was calling from the hall.

Jane said in a low, urgent tone, "Stay away. Please don't come."

She went out. Poirot heard the sounds of altercation. Heard Mrs. Olivera's high, complaining, clucking voice. "I really will not tolerate your rudeness, Jane. I shall take steps to see that you do not interfere—"

The secretary said, "Then at a little before six tomorrow, M. Poirot?"

Poirot nodded assent mechanically. He was standing like a man who has seen a ghost. But it was his ears, not his eyes, that had given him the shock.

Two of the sentences that had drifted in through the open door were almost identical with those he had heard last night through the telephone, and he knew why the voice had been faintly familiar.

As he walked out into the sunshine he shook his head blankly.

Mrs. Olivera?

But it was impossible! It could not have been *Mrs. Olivera* who had spoken over the phone!

That empty-headed society woman—selfish, brainless, grasping, self-centered? What had he called her to himself just now?

"That good fat hen? *C'est ridicule!*" said Hercule Poirot. His ears, he decided, must have deceived him. And yet—

The Rolls called punctually for Poirot at a little before six.

Alistair Blunt and his secretary were the only occupants. Mrs. Olivera and Jane had gone down in another car earlier, it seemed.

The drive was uneventful. Blunt talked a little, mostly of his garden and of a recent horticultural show.

Poirot congratulated him on his escape from death, at which Blunt demurred. He said, "Oh, *that!* Don't think the fellow was shooting at me particularly. Anyway, the poor chap hadn't the first idea of how to aim! Just one of these half-crazed students. There's no harm in them really. They just get worked up and fancy that a pot shot at the P.M. will alter the course of history. It's pathetic, really."

"There have been other attempts on your life, have there not?"

"Sounds quite melodramatic," said Blunt, with a slight twinkle. "Someone sent me a bomb by post not long ago. It wasn't a very efficient bomb. You know, these fellows who want to take on the management of the world—what sort of an efficient business do they think they could make of it, when they can't even devise an effectual bomb?"

He shook his head.

"It's always the same thing—long-haired, woolly idealists —without one practical bit of knowledge in their heads. I'm not a clever chap—never have been—but I can just read and write and do arithmetic. D'you understand what I mean by that?"

"I think so, but explain to me further."

"Well, if I read something that is written down in English *I can understand what it means*—I am not talking of abstruse stuff, formulae or philosophy—just plain business-like English—*most people can't!* If I want to write down something *I can write down what I mean*—I've discovered that quite a lot of people can't do that, either! And, as I say, I can do plain arithmetic. If Jones has eight bananas and Brown takes ten away from him, how many will Jones have left? That's the kind of sum people like to pretend has a simple answer. They won't admit, first, that Brown can't do it—and second, that there won't be an answer in plus bananas!"

"They prefer the answer to be a conjuring trick?"

"Exactly. Politicians are just as bad. But I've always held out for plain common sense. You can't beat it, you know, in the end."

He added with a slightly self-conscious laugh, "But I mustn't talk shop. Bad habit. Besides, I like to leave business matters behind when I get away from London. I've been looking forward, M. Poirot, to hearing a few of *your* adventures. I read a lot of thrillers and detective stories, you know. Do you think any of them are true to life?"

The conversation dwelt for the rest of the journey on the more spectacular cases of Hercule Poirot. Alistair Blunt displayed himself as avid as any schoolboy for details.

This pleasant atmosphere sustained a chill on arrival

at Exsham where behind her massive bust Mrs. Olivera radiated a freezing disapproval. She ignored Poirot as far as possible, addressing herself exclusively to her host and to Mr. Selby.

The latter showed Poirot to his room.

The house was a charming one, not very big, and furnished with the same quiet good taste that Poirot had noticed in London. Everything was costly but simple. The vast wealth that owned it was only indicated by the smoothness with which this apparent simplicity was produced. The service was admirable—the cooking English, not Continental—the wines at dinner stirred Poirot to a passion of appreciation. They had a perfect clear soup, a grilled sole, saddle of lamb with tiny young garden peas, and strawberries and cream.

Poirot was so enjoying these creature comforts that the continued frigid demeanor of Mrs. Olivera and the brusque rudeness of her daughter, hardly attracted his attention. Jane, for some reason, was regarding him with definite hostility. Hazily, toward the end of dinner, Poirot wondered why!

Looking down the table with mild curiosity, Blunt asked, "Helen not dining with us tonight?"

Julia Olivera's lips drew themselves in with a taut line. She said, "Dear Helen has been overtiring herself, I think, in the garden. I suggested it would be far better for her to go to bed and rest than to bother to dress herself up and come here. She quite saw my point."

"Oh, I see." Blunt looked vague and a little puzzled. "I thought it made a bit of a change for her at week-ends."

"Helen is such a simple soul. She likes turning in early," said Mrs. Olivera firmly.

When Poirot joined the ladies in the drawing-room, Blunt having remained behind for a few minutes' conversation with his secretary, he heard Jane Olivera say to her mother, "Uncle Alistair didn't quite like the cool way you'd shelved Helen Montressor, Mother."

"Nonsense," said Mrs. Olivera robustly. "Alistair is too good-natured. Poor relations are all very well—very kind of him to let her have the cottage rent free, but to think he has to have her up to the house every week-end for dinner is absurd! She's only a second cousin or something. I don't think Alistair ought to be imposed upon!"

"I think she's proud in her way," said Jane. "She does an awful lot in the garden."

"That shows a proper spirit," said Mrs. Olivera comfortably. "The Scotch are very independent and one respects them for it."

She settled herself comfortably on the sofa and, still not taking any notice of Poirot, added, "Just bring me the *Low Down Review*, dear. There's something about Lois Van Schuyler in it and that Moroccan guide of hers."

Alistair Blunt appeared in the doorway. He said, "Now, M. Poirot, come into my room."

Alistair Blunt's own sanctum was a low, long room at the back of the house, with windows opening upon the garden. It was comfortable, with deep armchairs and settees and just enough pleasant untidiness to make it livable.

Needless to say, Hercule Poirot would have preferred a greater symmetry!

After offering his guest a cigarette and lighting his own pipe, Alistair Blunt came to the point quite simply and directly.

He said, "There's a good deal that I'm not satisfied about. I'm referring, of course, to this Sainsbury Seale woman. For reasons of their own—reasons no doubt which are perfectly justified—the authorities have called off the hunt. I don't know exactly who Albert Chapman is or what he's doing—but whatever it is, it's something pretty vital and it's the sort of business that might land him in a tight spot. I don't know the ins and outs of it, but the

P.M. did just mention that they can't afford any publicity whatever about this case and that the sooner it fades out of the public's memory the better.

"That's quite okay. That's the official view, and they know what's necessary. So the police have got their hands tied."

He leaned forward in his chair.

"*But I want to know the truth, M. Poirot.* And you're the man to find it out for me. *You* aren't hampered by officialdom."

"What do you want me to do, M. Blunt?"

"I want you to find this woman—Sainsbury Seale."

"Alive or dead?"

Alistair Blunt's eyebrows rose.

"You think it possible that she is dead?"

Hercule Poirot was silent for a minute or two, then he said, speaking slowly and with weight, "If you want my opinion—but it is only an opinion, remember—then, yes, I think she is dead—"

"Why do you think so?"

Hercule Poirot smiled slightly.

He said, "It would not make sense to you if I said it was because of a pair of unworn stockings in a drawer."

Alistair Blunt stared at him curiously.

"You're an odd man, M. Poirot."

"I am very odd. That is to say, I am methodical, orderly, and logical—and I do not like distorting facts to support a theory—that, I find—*is* unusual!"

Alistair Blunt said, "I've been turning the whole thing over in my mind—it takes me a little time always to think a thing out. And the whole business is deuced odd! I mean —that dentist chap shooting himself, and then this Chapman woman packed away in her own fur chest with her face smashed in. It's nasty! It's damned nasty! I can't help feeling that there's something *behind* it all."

Poirot nodded.

Blunt said, "And you know—the more I think of it—I'm quite sure that woman never knew my wife. It was just a pretext to speak to *me*. But why? What good did it do her? I mean—bar a small subscription—and even that was made out to the society, not to her personally. And yet I do feel —that—that it was engineered—just meeting me on the steps of the house. It was all so pat. So suspiciously well-timed! But *why*? That's what I keep asking myself—why?"

"It is indeed the word—why? I, too, ask myself—and I cannot see it—no, I cannot see it."

"You've no ideas at all on the subject?"

Poirot waved an exasperated hand.

"My ideas are childish in the extreme. I tell myself, it was perhaps a ruse to indicate you to someone—to point you out. But that again is absurd—you are quite a well-known man—and anyway how much more simple to say, 'See, that is he—the man who entered now by that door.'"

"And anyway," said Blunt, "why *should* anyone want to point me out?"

"Mr. Blunt, think back once more on your time that morning in the dentist's chair. Did nothing that Morley said strike an unusual note? Is there nothing at all that you can remember which might help as a clue?"

Alistair Blunt frowned in an effort of memory. Then he shook his head. "I'm sorry. I can't think of anything."

"You're quite sure he didn't mention this woman—this Miss Sainsbury Seale?"

"No."

"Or the other woman—Mrs. Chapman?"

"No—no—we didn't speak of people at all. We mentioned roses, gardens needing rain, holidays—nothing else."

"And no one came into the room while you were there?"

"Let me see—no, I don't think so. On other occasions I seem to remember a young woman being there—fair-haired girl. But she wasn't there this time. Oh, another dentist fellow came in, I remember—fellow with an Irish accent."

"What did he say or do?"

"Just asked Morley some question and went out again. Morley was a bit short with him, I fancy. He was only there a minute or so."

"And there is nothing else you can remember? Nothing at all?"

"No. He was absolutely normal."

Hercule Poirot said thoughtfully, "I, too, found him absolutely normal."

There was a long pause. Then Poirot said, "Do you happen to remember, monsieur, a young man who was in the waiting-room downstairs with you that morning?"

Alistair Blunt frowned.

"Let me see—yes, there was a young man—rather restless he was. I don't remember him particularly, though. Why?"

"Would you know him again if you saw him?"

Blunt shook his head. "I hardly glanced at him."

"He didn't try to enter into conversation with you at all?"

"No." Blunt looked with frank curiosity at the other. "What's the point? Who is this young man?"

"His name is Howard Raikes."

Poirot watched keenly for any reaction, but he saw none.

"Ought I to know his name? Have I met him elsewhere?"

"I do not think you have met him. He is a friend of your niece, Miss Olivera's."

"Oh, one of Jane's friends."

"Her mother, I gather, does not approve of the friendship."

Alistair Blunt said absently, "I don't suppose that will cut any ice with Jane."

"So seriously does her mother regard the friendship that I gather she brought her daughter over from the States on purpose to get her away from this young man."

"Oh!" Blunt's face registered comprehension. "It's *that* fellow, is it?"

"Aha, you become more interested now."

"He's a most undesirable young fellow in every way, I believe. Mixed up in a lot of subversive activities."

"I understand from Miss Olivera that he made an appointment that morning in Queen Charlotte Street, solely in order to get a look at you."

"To try and get me to approve of him?"

"Well—no—I understand the idea was that *he* should be induced to approve of *you.*"

Alistair Blunt said indignantly, "Well, of all the damned cheek!"

Poirot concealed a smile. "It appears you are everything that he most disapproves of."

"He's certainly the kind of young man *I* disapprove of! Spends his time tub-thumping and talking hot air, instead of doing a decent job of work!"

Poirot was silent for a minute, then he said, "Will you forgive me if I ask you an impertinent and very personal question?"

"Fire ahead."

"In the event of your death, what are your testamentary dispositions?"

Blunt stared. He said sharply, "Why do you want to know that?"

"Because—it is just possible"—he shrugged his shoulders —"that it might be relevant to this case."

"Nonsense!"

"Perhaps. But perhaps not."

Alistair Blunt said coldly, "I think you are being unduly melodramatic, M. Poirot. Nobody has been trying to murder *me*—or anything like that!"

"A bomb on your breakfast table—a shot in the street—"

"Oh, those! Any man who deals in the world's finance in a big way is liable to that kind of attention from some crazy fanatic!"

"It might possibly be a case of someone who is not a fanatic and not crazy."

Blunt stared. "What are you driving at?"

"In plain language, I want to know who benefits by your death."

Blunt grinned. "Chiefly the St. Edward's Hospital, the Cancer Hospital, and the Royal Institute for the Blind."

"Ah!"

"In addition, I have left a sum of money to my niece by marriage, Mrs. Julia Olivera, an equivalent sum, but in trust, to her daughter, Jane Olivera, and also a substantial provision for my only surviving relative, a second cousin, Helen Montressor, who was left very badly off and who occupies a small cottage on the estate here."

He paused and then said, "This, M. Poirot, is strictly in confidence."

"Naturally, monsieur, naturally."

Alistair Blunt added sarcastically, "I suppose you do not suggest, M. Poirot, that either Julia or Jane Olivera, or my cousin, Helen Montressor, are planning to murder me for my money?"

"I suggest nothing—nothing at all."

Blunt's slight irritation subsided. He said, "And you'll take on that other commission for me?"

"The finding of Miss Sainsbury Seale? Yes, I will."

Alistair Blunt said heartily, "Good man."

In leaving the room Poirot almost cannoned into a tall figure outside the door.

He said, "I beg your pardon, mademoiselle."

Jane Olivera drew apart a little.

She said, "Do you know what I think of you, M. Poirot?"

"*Eh bien*—mademoiselle—"

She did not give him time to finish. The question, indeed, had but a rhetorical value. All that it meant was that Jane Olivera was to answer it herself.

"You're a spy, that's what you are! A miserable, low, snooping spy, nosing round and making trouble!"

"I assure you, mademoiselle—"

"I know just what you're after! And I know now just what lies you tell! Why don't you admit it straight out? Well, I'll tell you this—you won't find out *anything—anything* at all! There's nothing to find out! No one's going to harm a hair of my precious uncle's head. *He's* safe enough. He'll always be safe. Safe and smug and prosperous—and full of platitudes! He's just a stodgy John Bull, that's what he is—without an ounce of imagination or vision."

She paused; then, her agreeable, husky voice deepening, she said venomously, "I loathe the sight of you—you bloody little bourgeois detective!" She swept away from him in a whirl of expensive model drapery.

Hercule Poirot remained, his eyes very wide open, his eyebrows raised, and his hand thoughtfully caressing his mustaches.

The epithet bourgeois was, he admitted, well applied to him. His outlook on life was essentially bourgeois, and always had been, but the employment of it as an epithet of contempt by the exquisitely turned out Jane Olivera, gave him, as he expressed it to himself, furiously to think.

He went, still thinking, into the drawing-room.

Mrs. Olivera was playing patience.

She looked up as Poirot entered, surveyed him with the cold look she might have bestowed upon a black beetle, and murmured distantly, "Red knave on black queen."

Chilled, Poirot retreated. He reflected mournfully, *Alas, it would seem that nobody loves me!*

He strolled out through the window into the garden.

It was an enchanting evening with a smell of night-scented stocks in the air. Poirot sniffed happily and strolled along a path that ran between two herbaceous borders.

He turned a corner and two dimly seen figures sprang apart.

It would seem that he had interrupted a pair of lovers. Poirot hastily turned and retraced his steps.

Even out here, it would seem, his presence was *de trop*.

He passed Alistair Blunt's window and Alistair Blunt was dictating to Mr. Selby.

There seemed definitely only one place for Hercule Poirot.

He went up to his bedroom.

He pondered for some time on various fantastic aspects of the situation.

Had he or had he not made a mistake in believing the voice on the telephone to be that of Mrs. Olivera? Surely the idea was absurd!

He recalled the melodramatic revelations of quiet little Mr. Barnes. He speculated on the mysterious whereabouts of Mr. Q.X.912, alias Albert Chapman. He remembered, with a spasm of annoyance, the anxious look in the eyes of the maidservant, Agnes—

It was always the same way—people *would* keep things back! Usually quite unimportant things, but until they were cleared out of the way, impossible to pursue a straight path.

At the moment the path was anything but straight!

And the most unaccountable obstacle in the way of clear thinking and orderly progress was what he described to himself as the contradictory and impossible problem of Miss Sainsbury Seale. For, if the facts that Hercule Poirot had observed were true facts—then nothing whatever made sense!

Hercule Poirot said to himself, with astonishment in the thought, "Is it possible that I am growing old?"

Chapter Six

ELEVEN, TWELVE, MEN MUST DELVE

AFTER PASSING A TROUBLED NIGHT, Hercule Poirot was up and about early on the next day. The weather was perfect and he retraced his steps of last night.

The herbaceous borders were in full beauty and though Poirot himself leaned to a more orderly type of flower arrangement—a neat arrangement of beds of scarlet geraniums such as are seen at Ostend—he nevertheless realized that here was the perfection of the English garden spirit.

He pursued his way through a rose garden, where the neat layout of the beds delighted him—and through the winding ways of an alpine rock garden, coming at last to the walled kitchen gardens.

Here he observed a sturdy woman clad in a tweed coat and skirt, black-browed with short-cropped black hair who was talking in a slow, emphatic Scotch voice to what was evidently the head gardener. The head gardener, Poirot observed, did not appear to be enjoying the conversation.

A sarcastic inflection made itself heard in Miss Helen Montressor's voice, and Poirot escaped nimbly down a side path.

A gardener who had been, Poirot shrewdly suspected, resting on his spade, began digging with fervor. Poirot approached nearer. The man, a young fellow, dug with ardor, his back to Poirot, who paused to observe him.

"Good morning," said Poirot amiably.

A muttered "Morning, sir," was the response, but the man did not stop working.

Poirot was a little surprised. In his experience a gardener, though anxious to appear zealously at work as you approached, was usually only too willing to pause and pass the time of day when directly addressed.

It seemed, he thought, a little unnatural. He stood there for some minutes, watching the toiling figure. Was there, or was there not, something a little familiar about the turn of those shoulders? Or could it be, thought Hercule Poirot, that he was getting into a habit of thinking that both voices and shoulders were familiar when they were really nothing of the kind? Was he, as he had feared last night, growing old?

He passed thoughtfully onward out of the walled garden and paused to regard a rising slope of shrubbery outside.

Presently, like some fantastic moon, a round object rose gently over the top of the kitchen garden wall. It was the egg-shaped head of Hercule Poirot, and the eyes of Hercule Poirot regarded with a good deal of interest the face of the young gardener who had now stopped digging and was passing a sleeve across his wet face.

"Very curious and very interesting," murmured Hercule Poirot as he discreetly lowered his head once more.

He emerged from the shrubbery and brushed off some twigs and leaves that were spoiling the neatness of his apparel.

Yes, indeed, very curious and interesting that Frank Carter, who had a secretarial job in the country, should be working as a gardener in the employment of Alistair Blunt.

Reflecting on these points, Hercule Poirot heard a gong in the distance and retraced his steps toward the house.

On the way there he encountered his host talking to Miss Montressor who had just emerged from the kitchen garden by the farther door.

Her voice, with its Scotch burr, rose clear and distinct.

"It's verra kind of you, Alistairr, but I would preferr not to accept any invitations this week while yourr American relations are with you!"

Blunt said, "Julia's rather a tactless woman, but she doesn't mean—"

Miss Montressor said calmly, "In my opinion her manner to me is verra insolent, and I will not put up with insolence—from Amerrican women or any others!"

Miss Montressor moved away, Poirot came up to find Alistair Blunt looking as sheepish as most men look who are having trouble with their female relations.

He said ruefully, "Women really are the devil! Good morning, M. Poirot. Lovely day, isn't it?" They turned toward the house and Blunt said with a sigh, "I do miss my wife!"

In the dining-room, he remarked to the redoubtable Julia, "I'm afraid, Julia, you've rather hurt Helen's feelings."

Mrs. Olivera said grimly, "The Scotch are always touchy."

Alistair Blunt looked unhappy.

Hercule Poirot said, "You have a young gardener, I noticed, whom I think you must have taken on recently."

"I daresay," said Blunt. "Yes, Burton, my third gardener, left about three weeks ago, and we took this fellow on instead."

"Do you remember where he came from?"

"I really don't. MacAlister engaged him. Somebody or other asked me to give him a trial, I think. Recommended him warmly. I'm rather surprised, because MacAlister says he isn't much good. He wants to sack him."

"What is his name?"

"Dunning—Sunbury—something like that."

"Would it be a great impertinence to ask what you pay him?"

Alistair Blunt looked amused.

"Not at all. Two pounds fifteen, I think it is."

"Not more?"

"Certainly not more—might be a bit less."

"Now that," said Poirot, "is very curious."

Alistair Blunt looked at him inquiringly.

But Jane Olivera, rustling the paper, distracted the conversation.

"A lot of people seem out for your blood, Uncle Alistair!"

"Oh, you're reading the debate in the house. That's all right. Only Archerton—he's always tilting at windmills. And he's got the most crazy ideas of finance. If we let him have his way, England would be bankrupt in a week."

Jane said, "Don't you ever *want* to try anything new?"

"Not unless it's an improvement on the old, my dear."

"But you'd never think it would be. You'd always say, 'This would never work'—without even trying."

"Experimentalists can do a lot of harm."

"Yes, but how can you be satisfied with things as they are? All the waste and the inequality and the unfairness. Something *must* be done about it!"

"We get along pretty well in this country, Jane, all things considered."

Jane said passionately, "What's needed is a new heaven and a new earth! And you sit there eating kidneys!"

She got up and went out by the French window into the garden.

Alistair looked mildly surprised and a little uncomfortable.

He said, "Jane has changed a lot lately. Where does she get all these ideas?"

"Take no notice of what Jane says," said Mrs. Olivera. "Jane's a very silly girl. You know what girls are—they go to these queer parties in studios where the young men have funny ties and they come home and talk a lot of nonsense."

"Yes, but Jane was always rather a hard-boiled young woman."

"It's just a fashion, Alistair, these things are in the air!"

Alistair Blunt said, "Yes, they're in the air all right."

He looked a little worried.

Mrs. Olivera rose and Poirot opened the door for her. She swept out frowning.

Alistair Blunt said suddenly, "I don't like it, you know! Everybody's talking this sort of stuff! And it doesn't mean anything! It's all hot air! I find myself up against it the whole time—a new heaven and a new earth. What does it *mean?* They can't tell you themselves! They're just drunk on words."

He smiled suddenly, rather ruefully.

"I'm one of the last of the Old Guard, you know."

Poirot said curiously, "If you were—removed, what would happen?"

"Removed! What a way of putting it!" His face grew suddenly grave. "I'll tell you. A lot of damned fools would try a lot of very costly experiments. And that would be the end of stability—of common sense, of solvency. In fact, of this England of ours as we know it."

Poirot nodded his head. He was essentially in sympathy with the banker. He, too, approved of solvency. And he began to realize with a new meaning exactly just what Alistair Blunt stood for. Mr. Barnes had told him, but he had hardly taken it in then. Quite suddenly, he was afraid.

"I've finished my letters," said Blunt, appearing later in the morning. "Now, M. Poirot, I'm going to show you my garden."

The two men went out together and Blunt talked eagerly of his hobby.

The rock garden, with its rare alpine plants, was his greatest joy and they spent some time there while Blunt pointed out certain minute and rare species.

Hercule Poirot, his feet encased in his best patent-leather shoes, listened patiently, shifting his weight tenderly from one foot to the other and wincing slightly as the heat of the sun caused the illusion that his feet were gigantic puddings!

His host strolled on, pointing out various plants in the wide border. Bees were humming and from near at hand came the monotonous clicking of a pair of shears trimming a laurel hedge.

It was all very drowsy and peaceful.

Blunt paused at the end of the border, looking back. The clip of the shears was quite close by, though the clipper was concealed from view.

"Look at the vista down from here, Poirot. The sweet Williams are particularly fine this year. I don't know when I've seen them so good—and those are Russell lupines. Marvelous colors."

Crack! The shot broke the peace of the morning. Something sang angrily through the air. Alistair Blunt turned bewildered to where a faint thread of smoke was rising from the middle of the laurels.

There was a sudden outcry of angry voices, the laurels heaved as two men struggled together. A high-pitched American voice sang out resolutely, "I've got you, you damned scoundrel! Drop that gun!"

Two men struggled out into the open. The young gardener who had dug so industriously that morning was writhing in the powerful grip of a man nearly a head taller.

Poirot recognized the latter at once. He had already guessed from the voice.

Frank Carter snarled, "Let go of me! It wasn't me, I tell you! I never did."

Howard Raikes said, "Oh no? Just shooting at the birds, I suppose!"

He stopped—looking at the newcomers.

"Mr. Alistair Blunt? This guy here has just taken a pot shot at you. I caught him right in the act."

Frank Carter cried out, "It's a lie! I was clipping the

hedge. I heard a shot and the gun fell right here at my feet. I picked it up—that's only natural, that is, and then this bloke jumped on me."

Howard Raikes said grimly, "The gun was in your hand and it had just been fired!"

With a final gesture, he tossed the pistol to Poirot.

"Let's see what the dick's got to say about it! Lucky I got hold of you in time. I guess there are several more shots in that automatic of yours."

Poirot murmured, "Precisely."

Blunt was frowning angrily. He said sharply, "Now then, Dunnon—Dunbury—what's your name?"

Hercule Poirot interrupted. He said, "This man's name is Frank Carter."

Carter turned on him furiously.

"You've had it in for me all along! You came spying on me that Sunday. I tell you, it's not true. I never shot at him."

Hercule Poirot said gently, "Then, in that case, *who did?*"

He added, "There is no one else here but ourselves, you see."

Jane Olivera came running along the path. Her hair streamlined back behind her. Her eyes were wide with fear. She gasped, "Howard?"

Howard Raikes said lightly, "Hullo, Jane. I've just been saving your uncle's life."

"Oh!" She stopped. *"You* have?"

"Your arrival certainly seems to have been very opportune, Mr.—er—" Blunt hesitated.

"This is Howard Raikes, Uncle Alistair. He's a friend of mine."

Blunt looked at Raikes—he smiled.

"Oh!" he said. "So you are Jane's young man! I must thank you."

With a puffing noise as of a steam engine at high pressure Julia Olivera appeared on the scene. She panted out, "I heard a shot. Is Alistair— Why—" She stared blankly at Howard Raikes. *"You?* Why, why, how *dare* you?"

Jane said in an icy voice, "Howard has just saved Uncle Alistair's life, Mother."

"What? I—I—"

"This man tried to shoot Uncle Alistair and Howard grabbed him and took the pistol away from him."

Frank Carter said violently, "You're bloody liars, all of you."

Mrs. Olivera, her jaw dropping, said blankly, "Oh!" It took her a minute or two to readjust her poise. She turned first to Blunt.

"My dear Alistair! How *awful!* Thank God you're safe. But it must have been a frightful shock. I—I feel quite faint myself. I wonder—do you think I could have just a *little* brandy?"

Blunt said quickly, "Of course. Come back to the house."

She took his arm, leaning on it heavily.

Blunt looked over his shoulder at Poirot and Howard Raikes.

"Can you bring that fellow along?" he asked. "We'll ring up the police and hand him over."

Frank Carter opened his mouth, but no words came. He was dead white, and his knees were wilting. Howard Raikes hauled him along with an unsympathetic hand.

"Come on, *you,*" he said.

Frank Carter murmured hoarsely and unconvincingly, "It's all a lie—"

Howard Raikes looked at Poirot.

"You've got precious little to say for yourself for a high-toned sleuth! Why don't you throw your weight about a bit?"

"I am reflecting, Mr. Raikes."

"I guess you'll need to reflect! I should say you'll lose your job over this! It isn't thanks to *you* that Alistair Blunt is still alive at this minute."

"This is your second good deed of the kind, is it not, Mr. Raikes?"

"What the hell do you mean?"

"It was only yesterday, was it not, that you caught and held the man whom you believed to have shot at Mr. Blunt and the Prime Minister?"

Howard Raikes said, "Er—yes. I seem to be making a kind of habit of it."

"But there is a difference," Hercule Poirot pointed out. "Yesterday, the man you caught and held was *not* the man who fired the shot in question. You made a mistake."

Frank Carter said sullenly, "He's made a mistake now."

"Quiet, you," said Raikes.

Hercule Poirot murmured to himself, "I wonder—"

Dressing for dinner, adjusting his tie to an exact symmetry, Hercule Poirot frowned at his reflection in the mirror.

He was dissatisfied—but he would have been at a loss to explain why. For the case, as he owned to himself, was so very clear. Frank Carter had indeed been caught red-handed.

It was not as though he had any particular belief in, or liking for, Frank Carter. Carter, he thought dispassionately, was definitely what the English call a "wrong 'un." He was an unpleasant young bully of the kind that appeals to women, so that they are reluctant to believe the worst however plain the evidence.

And Carter's whole story was weak in the extreme. This tale of having been approached by agents of the secret service—and offered a plummy job. To take the post of gardener and report on the conversations and actions of the other gardeners. It was a story that was disproved easily enough—there was no foundation for it.

A particularly weak invention—the kind of thing, Poirot reflected, that a man like Carter *would* invent.

And on Carter's side, there was nothing at all to be said. He could offer no alternative explanation, except that somebody else must have shot off the revolver. He kept repeating that. It was a frame-up.

No, there was nothing to be said for Carter except, perhaps, that it seemed an odd coincidence that Howard Raikes should have been present two days running at the moment when a bullet had just missed Alistair Blunt.

But presumably there wasn't anything in that. Raikes certainly hadn't fired the shot in Downing Street. And his presence down here was fully accounted for—he had come down to be near his girl. No, there was nothing definitely improbable in *his* story.

It had turned out, of course, very fortunately for Howard Raikes. When a man has just saved you from a bullet, you cannot forbid him the house. The least you can do is to show friendliness and extend hospitality. Mrs. Olivera didn't like it, obviously, but even she saw that there was nothing to be done about it.

Jane's undesirable young man had got his foot in and he meant to keep it there!

Poirot watched him speculatively during the evening.

He was playing his part with a good deal of astuteness. He did not air any subversive views, he kept off politics. He told amusing stories of his hitchhikes and tramps in wild places.

He is no longer the wolf, thought Poirot. *No, he has put on the sheep's clothing. But underneath? I wonder—*

As Poirot was preparing for bed that night, there was a rap on the door. Poirot called, "Come in," and Howard Raikes entered.

He laughed at Poirot's expression.

"Surprised to see me? I've had my eye on you all evening. I didn't like the way you were looking. Kind of thoughtful."

"Why should that worry you, my friend?"

"I don't know why, but it did. I thought maybe that you were finding certain things just a bit hard to swallow."

"Eh bien? And if so?"

"Well, I decided that I'd best come clean. About yesterday, I mean. That was a fake show all right! You see, I was watching his lordship come out of Ten Downing Street and I saw Ram Lal fire at him. I know Ram Lal. He's a nice kid. A bit excitable but he feels the wrongs of India very keenly. Well, there was no harm done, that precious pair of stuffed shirts weren't harmed—the bullet had missed 'em both by miles—so I decided to put up a show and hope the Indian kid would get clear. I grabbed hold of a shabby little guy just by me and called out that I'd got the villain and hoped Ram Lal was beating it all right. But the dicks were too smart. They were onto him in a flash. That's just how it was. See?"

Hercule Poirot said, "And today?"

"That's different. There weren't any Ram Lals about today. Carter was the only man on the spot. *He* fired that pistol all right! It was still in his hand when I jumped on him. He was going to try a second shot, I expect."

Poirot said, "You were very anxious to preserve the safety of M. Blunt?"

Raikes grinned—an engaging grin.

"A bit odd, you think, after all I've said? Oh, I admit it. I think Blunt is a guy who *ought* to be shot—for the sake of progress and humanity—I don't mean personally—he's a nice enough old boy in his British way. I think that, and yet when I saw someone taking a pot shot at him I leaped in and interfered. That shows you how illogical the human animal is. It's crazy, isn't it?"

"The gap between theory and practice is a wide one."

"I'll say it is!" Mr. Raikes got up from the bed where

he had been sitting.

His smile was easy and confiding.

"I just thought," he said, "that I'd come along and explain the thing to you."

He went out, shutting the door carefully behind him.

" 'Deliver me, O Lord, from the evil man, and preserve me from the wicked man,' " sang Mrs. Olivera in a firm voice, slightly off the note.

There was a relentlessness about her enunciation of the sentiment which made Hercule Poirot deduce that Mr. Howard Raikes was the wicked man immediately in her mind.

Hercule Poirot had accompanied his host and the family to the morning service in the village church.

Howard Raikes had said with a faint sneer, "So you always go to church, Mr. Blunt?"

And Alistair had murmured vaguely something about it being expected of you in the country—can't let the parson down, you know—which typically English sentiment had merely bewildered the young man, and had made Hercule Poirot smile comprehendingly.

Mrs. Olivera had tactfully accompanied her host and commanded Jane to do likewise.

" 'They have sharpened their tongues like a serpent,' " sang the choir boys in shrill treble, " 'adder's poison is under their lips.' "

The tenors and basses demanded with gusto, " 'Keep me, O Lord, from the hands of the ungodly. Preserve me from the wicked men who are purposed to overthrow my goings.' "

Hercule Poirot essayed a hesitant baritone.

" 'The proud have laid a snare for me,' " he sang, " 'and spread a net with cords: yea, and set traps in my way—' "

His mouth remained open.

He saw it—saw clearly the trap into which he had so

nearly fallen!

A snare cunningly laid—a net with cords—a pit open at his feet—dug carefully so that he should fall into it.

Like a man in a trance Hercule Poirot remained, mouth open, staring into space. He remained there as the congregation seated themselves with a rustle; until Jane Olivera tugged at his arm and murmured a sharp, "Sit down."

Hercule Poirot sat down. An aged clergyman with a beard intoned, "Here beginneth the fifteenth chapter of the First Book of Samuel," and began to read.

But Poirot heard nothing of the smiting of the Amalekites.

He was in a daze—a glorious daze where isolated facts spun wildly round before settling neatly into their appointed places.

It was like a kaleidoscope—shoe buckles, size nine stockings, a damaged face, the low tastes in literature of Alfred the page boy, the activities of Mr. Amberiotis, and the part played by the late Mr. Morley, all rose up and whirled and settled themselves down into a coherent pattern.

For the first time, Hercule Poirot was looking at the case *the right way up.*

" 'For rebellion is as the sin of witchcraft and stubbornness is as iniquity and idolatry. Because thou hast rejected the word of the Lord, he hath also rejected thee from being king.' Here endeth the first lesson," quavered the aged clergyman all in one breath.

As one in a dream, Hercule Poirot rose to praise the Lord in the *Te Deum.*

Chapter Seven

Thirteen, Fourteen, Maids Are Courting

"M. REILLY, IS IT NOT?" The young Irishman started as the voice spoke at his elbow.

He turned.

Standing next to him at the counter of the shipping company was a small man with large mustaches and an egg-shaped head.

"You do not remember me, perhaps?"

"You do yourself an injustice, M. Poirot. You're not a man who's easily forgotten."

He turned back to speak to the clerk who was waiting behind the counter.

The voice at his elbow murmured, "You are going abroad for a holiday?"

"It's not a holiday I'm taking. And you yourself, M. Poirot? You're not turning your back on this country, I hope?"

"Sometimes," said Hercule Poirot, "I return for a short while to my own country—Belgium."

"I'm going farther than that," said Reilly. "It's America for me." He added, "And I don't think I'll be coming back, either."

"I'm sorry to hear that, Mr. Reilly. You are, then, abandoning your practice in Queen Charlotte Street?"

"If you'd say it was abandoning me, you'd be nearer the mark."

"Indeed? That is very sad."

"It doesn't worry me. When I think of the debts I shall leave behind me unpaid, I'm a happy man."

He grinned engagingly.

"It's not I who'll be shooting myself because of money

troubles. Leave them behind you, I say, and start afresh. I've got my qualifications and they're good ones if I say so myself."

Poirot murmured, "I saw Miss Morley the other day."

"Was that a pleasure to you? I'd say it was not. A more sour-faced woman never lived. I've often wondered what she'd be like drunk—but that's what no one will ever know."

Poirot said, "Did you agree with the verdict of the coroner's court on your partner's death?"

"I did not," said Reilly emphatically.

"You don't think he made a mistake in the injection?"

Reilly said, "If Morley injected that Greek with the amount that they say he did, he was either drunk or else he meant to kill the man. And I've never seen Morley drink."

"So you think it was deliberate?"

"I'd not like to be saying that. It's a grave accusation to be making. Truly now, I don't believe it."

"There must be some explanation."

"There must indeed—but I've not thought of it yet."

Poirot said, "When did you last actually see Mr. Morley alive?"

"Let me see now. It's a long time after to be asking me a thing like that. It would be the night before—about a quarter to seven."

"You didn't see him on the actual day of the murder?"

Reilly shook his head.

"You are sure?" Poirot persisted.

"Oh, I'd not say that. But I don't remember—"

"You did not, for instance, go up to his room about eleven thirty-five when he had a patient there."

"You're right now. I did. There was a technical question I had to ask him about some instruments I was ordering. They'd rung me up about it. But I was only there for a minute, so it slipped my memory. He had a patient there at the time."

Poirot nodded. He said, "There is another question I always meant to ask you. Your patient, Mr. Raikes, canceled his appointment by walking out. What did you do during that half hour's leisure?"

"What I always do when I have any leisure. Mixed myself a drink. And as I've been telling you, I put through a telephone call and ran up to see Morley for a minute."

Poirot said, "And I also understand that you had no patient from half past twelve to one after Mr. Barnes left. When did he leave, by the way?"

"Oh! Just after half past twelve."

"And what did you do then?"

"The same as before. Mixed myself another drink!"

"And went up to see Morley again?"

Mr. Reilly smiled.

"Are you meaning did I go up and shoot him? I've told you already, long ago, that I did not. But you've only my word for it."

Poirot said, "What did you think of the house-parlor-maid, Agnes?"

Reilly stared. "Now that's a funny question to be asking."

"But I should like to know."

"I'll answer you. I didn't think about her. Georgina kept a strict eye on the maids—and quite right, too. The girl never looked my way once—which was bad taste on her part."

"I have a feeling," said Hercule Poirot, "that that girl knows something."

He looked inquiringly at Mr. Reilly. The latter smiled and shook his head.

"Don't ask me," he said. "I know nothing about it. I can't help you at all."

He gathered up the tickets which were lying in front of him and went off with a nod and a smile.

Poirot explained to a disillusioned clerk that he would not make up his mind about that cruise to the Northern Capitals after all.

Poirot paid another visit to Hampstead. Mrs. Adams was a little surprised, perhaps, to see him. Though he had been vouched for, so to speak, by a Chief Inspector of Scotland Yard, she nevertheless regarded him as a "quaint little foreigner" and had not taken his pretensions very seriously. She was, however, very willing to talk.

After the first sensational announcement about the identity of the victim, the findings of the inquest had received little publicity. It had been a case of mistaken identity—the body of Mrs. Chapman had been mistaken for that of Miss Sainsbury Seale. That was all that the public knew. The fact that Miss Sainsbury Seale had been probably the last person to see the unfortunate Mrs. Chapman alive was not stressed. There had been no hint in the press that Miss Sainsbury Seale might possibly be wanted by the police on a criminal charge.

Mrs. Adams had been very relieved when she knew that it was not her friend's body which had been discovered so dramatically. She appeared to have no idea that any suspicion might attach to Mabelle Sainsbury Seale.

"But it is so extraordinary that she has disappeared like this. I feel sure, M. Poirot, that it *must* be loss of memory."

Poirot said that it was very probable. He had known cases of the kind.

"Yes—I remember a friend of one of my cousins. She'd had a lot of nursing and worry, and it brought it on. Amnesia, I think they called it."

Poirot said that he believed that that was the technical term.

He paused and then asked if Mrs. Adams had ever heard Miss Sainsbury Seale speak of a Mrs. Albert Chapman.

No, Mrs. Adams never remembered her friend mentioning anyone of that name. But then, of course, it wasn't likely that Miss Sainsbury Seale should happen to mention everyone with whom she was acquainted. Who was this Mrs. Chapman? Had the police any idea who could have murdered her?

"It is still a mystery, madame." Poirot shook his head and then asked if it was Mrs. Adams who had recommended Mr. Morley as a dentist to Miss Sainsbury Seale.

Mrs. Adams replied in the negative. She herself went to a Mr. French in Harley Street and if Mabelle had asked her about a dentist, she would have sent her to him.

Possibly, Poirot thought, it might have been this Mrs. Chapman who recommended Miss Sainsbury Seale to go to Mr. Morley.

Mrs. Adams agreed that it might have been. Didn't they know at the dentist's?

But Poirot had already asked Miss Nevill that question and Miss Nevill had not known or had not remembered. She recollected Mrs. Chapman, but did not think the latter had ever mentioned a Miss Sainsbury Seale—the name being an odd one, she would have remembered it had she heard it then.

Poirot persevered with his questions.

Mrs. Adams had known Miss Sainsbury Seale first in India, had she not? Mrs. Adams agreed.

Did Mrs. Adams know if Miss Sainsbury Seale had met Mr. or Mrs. Alistair Blunt at any time out there?

"Oh, I don't think so, M. Poirot. You mean the big banker? They were out some years ago staying with the Viceroy, but I'm sure if Mabelle had met them at all, she would have talked about it or mentioned them.

"I'm afraid," added Mrs. Adams, with a faint smile, "one does usually mention the important people. We're all such snobs at heart."

"She never did mention the Blunts—Mrs. Blunt in particular?"

"Never."

"If she had been a close friend of Mrs. Blunt's probably you would have known?"

"Oh, yes. I don't believe she knew anyone like that. Mabelle's friends were all very ordinary people—like us."

"That, madame, I cannot allow," said Poirot gallantly.

Mrs. Adams went on talking of Mabelle Sainsbury Seale as one talks of a friend who has recently died. She recalled all Mabelle's good works, her kindnesses, her indefatigable work for the mission, her zeal, her earnestness.

Hercule Poirot listened. As Japp had said, Mabelle Sainsbury Seale was a real person. She had lived in Calcutta and taught elocution and worked among the native population. She had been respectable, well-meaning, a little fussy and stupid perhaps, but also what is termed a woman with a heart of gold.

And Mrs. Adams's voice ran on. "She was so much in *earnest* over everything, M. Poirot. And she found people so apathetic—so hard to rouse. It was very difficult to get subscriptions out of people—worse every year, with the income tax rising and the cost of living and everything. She said to me once, 'When one knows what money can do—the wonderful good you can accomplish with it—well, really, sometimes, Alice, I feel I would commit a *crime* to get it.' That shows, doesn't it, M. Poirot, how strongly she felt?"

"She said that, did she?" said Poirot thoughtfully.

He asked, casually, when Miss Sainsbury Seale had enunciated this particular statement, and learned that it had been about three months ago.

He left the house and walked away lost in thought.

He was considering the character of Mabelle Sainsbury Seale.

A nice woman—an earnest and kindly woman—a respectable, decent type of woman. It was among that type of person that Mr. Barnes had suggested a potential criminal could be found.

She had traveled back on the same boat from India as Mr. Amberiotis. There seemed reason to believe that she had lunched with him at the Savoy.

She had accosted and claimed acquaintance with Alistair Blunt and laid claim to an intimacy with his wife.

She had twice visited King Leopold Mansions where, later, a dead body had been found dressed in her clothes and with her handbag conveniently identifying it.

A little *too* convenient, that!

She had left the Glengowrie Court Hotel suddenly after an interview with the police.

Could the theory that Hercule Poirot believed to be true account for and explain all those facts?

He thought it could.

These meditations had occupied Hercule Poirot on his homeward way until he reached Regent's Park. He decided to traverse a part of the park on foot before taking a taxi. By experience, he knew to a nicety the moment when his smart patent-leather shoes began to press painfully on his feet.

It was a lovely summer's day and Poirot looked indulgently on courting nursemaids and their swains, laughing and giggling while their chubby charges profited by nurse's inattention.

Dogs barked and romped.

Little boys sailed boats.

And under nearly every tree was a couple sitting close together.

"Ah! *Jeunesse, jeunesse,*" murmured Hercule Poirot, pleasurably affected by the sight.

They were chic, these little London girls. They wore their tawdry clothes with an air.

Their figures, however, he considered lamentably deficient. Where were the rich curves, the voluptuous lines that had formerly delighted the eye of an admirer?

He, Hercule Poirot, remembered women. One woman, in particular—what a sumptuous creature—a Bird of Paradise—a Venus—

What woman was there among these pretty chits nowadays, who could hold a candle to Countess Vera Rossakoff? A genuine Russian aristocrat, an aristocrat to her finger tips! And also, he remembered, a most accomplished thief— One of those natural geniuses—

With a sigh, Poirot wrenched his thoughts away from the flamboyant creature of his dreams.

It was not only, he noted, the little nursemaids and their like who were being wooed under the trees of Regent's Park.

That was a Schiaparelli creation there, under that lime tree, with the young man who bent his head so close to hers, who was pleading so earnestly.

One must not yield too soon! He hoped the girl understood that. The pleasure of the chase must be extended as long as possible—

His beneficent eye still on them, he became suddenly aware of a familiarity in those two figures.

So Jane Olivera had come to Regent's Park to meet her young American revolutionary?

His face grew suddenly sad and rather stern.

After only a brief hesitation he crossed the grass to them.

Sweeping off his hat with a flourish, he said, *"Bonjour, mademoiselle."*

Jane Olivera, he thought, was not entirely displeased to see him.

Howard Raikes, on the other hand, was a good deal annoyed at the interruption.

He growled, "Oh, so it's *you* again!"

"Good afternoon, M. Poirot," said Jane. "How unexpectedly you always pop up, don't you?"

"Kind of a Jack-in-the-box," said Raikes, still eyeing

Poirot with considerable coldness.

"I do not intrude?" Poirot asked anxiously.

Jane Olivera said kindly, "Not at all."

Howard Raikes said nothing.

"It is a pleasant spot you have found here," said Poirot.

"It was," said Mr. Raikes.

Jane said, "Be quiet, Howard. You need to learn manners!"

Howard Raikes snorted and asked, "What's the good of manners?"

"You'll find they kind of help you along," said Jane. "*I* haven't got any myself, but that doesn't matter so much. To begin with I'm rich, and I'm moderately good-looking, and I've got a lot of influential friends—and none of those unfortunate disabilities they talk about so freely in the advertisements nowadays. I can get along all right without manners."

Raikes said, "I'm not in the mood for small talk, Jane. I guess I'll take myself off."

He got up, nodded curtly to Poirot, and strode away.

Jane Olivera stared after him, her chin cupped in her palm.

Poirot said with a sigh, "Alas, the proverb is true. When you are courting, two is company, is it not, three is none?"

Jane said, "Courting? What a word!"

"But yes, it is the right word, is it not? For a young man who pays attention to a young lady before asking her hand in marriage? They say, do they not, a courting couple?"

"Your friends seem to say some very funny things."

Hercule Poirot chanted softly, *"Thirteen, fourteen, maids are courting.* See, all around us they are doing it."

Jane said sharply, "Yes—I'm just one of a crowd, I suppose—"

She turned suddenly to Poirot.

"I want to apologize to you. I made a mistake the other day. I thought you had wormed your way in and come down to Exsham just to spy on Howard. But afterward Uncle Alistair told me that he had definitely asked you because he wanted you to clear up this business of that missing woman—Sainsbury Seale. That's right, isn't it?"

"Absolutely."

"So I'm sorry for what I said to you that evening. But it did look like it, you know. I mean—as though you *were* just following Howard and spying on us both."

"Even if it were true, mademoiselle—I was an excellent witness to the fact that Mr. Raikes bravely saved your uncle's life by springing on his assailant and preventing him from firing another shot."

"You've got a funny way of saying things, M. Poirot. I never know whether you're serious or not."

Poirot said gravely, "At the moment I am very serious, Miss Olivera."

Jane said with a slight break in her voice, "Why do you look at me like that? As though—as though you were sorry for me?"

"Perhaps because I am sorry, mademoiselle, for the things that I shall have to do so soon—"

"Well, then—don't do them!"

"Alas, mademoiselle, but I must—"

She stared at him for a minute or two, then she said, "Have you—found that woman?"

Poirot said, "Let us say—*that I know where she is.*"

"Is she dead?"

"I have not said so."

"She's alive, then?"

"I have not said that, either."

Jane looked at him with irritation. She exclaimed, "Well, she's got to be one or the other, hasn't she?"

"Actually, it is not quite so simple."

"I believe you just *like* making things difficult!"

"It has been said of me," admitted Hercule Poirot.

Jane shivered. She said, "Isn't it funny? It's a lovely

warm day—and yet I suddenly feel cold—"

"Perhaps you had better walk on, mademoiselle."

Jane rose to her feet. She stood a minute irresolute. She said abruptly, "Howard wants me to marry him. At once. Without letting anyone know. He says—he says it's the only way I'll ever do it—that I'm weak—" She broke off, then with one hand she gripped Poirot's arm with surprising strength. "What shall I do about it, M. Poirot?"

"Why ask me to advise you? There are those who are nearer!"

"Mother? She'd scream the house down at the bare idea! Uncle Alistair? He'd be cautious and prosy. 'Plenty of time, my dear. Got to make quite sure, you know. Bit of an odd fish—this young man of yours. No sense in rushing things—' "

"Your friends?" suggested Poirot.

"I haven't got any friends. Only a silly crowd I drink and dance and talk inane catchwords with! Howard's the only *real* person I've ever come up against."

"Still—why ask *me*, Miss Olivera?"

Jane said, "Because you've got a queer look on your face—as though you were sorry about something—as though you knew something that—that—was—*coming*—"

She stopped.

"Well?" she demanded. "What do you say?"

Hercule Poirot slowly shook his head.

When Poirot reached home, George said, "Chief Inspector Japp is here, sir."

Japp grinned in a rueful way as Poirot came into the room.

"Here I am, old boy. Come round to say aren't you a marvel? How do you do it? What makes you think of these things?"

"All this meaning? But *pardon*, you will have some refreshment? Wine? Or perhaps the whisky?"

"The whisky is good enough for me."

A few minutes later he raised his glass, observing, "Here's to Hercule Poirot who is always right!"

"No, no, *mon ami.*"

"Here we had a lovely case of suicide. H. P. says it's murder—wants it to be murder—and dash it all, it *is* murder!"

"Ah? So you agree at last?"

"Well, nobody can say I'm pigheaded. I don't fly in the face of evidence. The trouble was there *wasn't* any evidence before."

"But there is now?"

"Yes, and I've come round to make the *amende honorable,* as you call it, and present the tidbit to you on toast, as it were."

"I am all agog, my good Japp."

"All right. Here goes. The pistol that Frank Carter tried to shoot Blunt with on Saturday is a twin pistol to the one that killed Morley!"

Poirot stared. "But that is extraordinary!"

"Yes, it makes it look rather black for Master Frank."

"It is not conclusive."

"No, but it's enough to make us reconsider the suicide verdict. They're a foreign make of pistol and rather uncommon at that!"

Hercule Poirot stared. His eyebrows looked like crescent moons. He said at last, "Frank Carter? No—surely not!"

Japp breathed a sigh of exasperation.

"What's the matter with you, Poirot? First you will have it that Morley was murdered and that it wasn't suicide. Then when I come and tell you we're inclined to come round to your view you hem and haw and don't seem to like it."

"You really believe that Morley was murdered by Frank Carter?"

"It fits. Carter had got a grudge against Morley—that

we knew all along. He came to Queen Charlotte Street that morning—and he pretended afterward that he had come along to tell his young woman he'd got a job—but we've now discovered that he *hadn't* got the job then. He didn't get it till later in the day. He admits that now. So there's lie Number One. He can't account for where he was at twenty-five past twelve onward. Says he was walking in the Marylebone Road, but the first thing he can prove is having a drink in a pub at five past one. And the barman says he was in a regular state—his hand shaking and his face as white as a sheet!"

Hercule Poirot sighed and shook his head. He murmured, "It does not accord with my ideas."

"What are these ideas of yours?"

"It is very disturbing what you tell me. Very disturbing indeed. Because, you see, if you are right—"

The door opened softly and George murmured deferentially, "Excuse me, sir, but—"

He got no further. Miss Gladys Nevill thrust him aside and came agitatedly into the room. She was crying.

"Oh, M. Poirot—"

"Here, I'll be off," said Japp hurriedly.

He left the room precipitately.

Gladys Nevill paid his back the tribute of a venomous look.

"That's the man—that horrid inspector from Scotland Yard—it's he who has trumped up a whole case against poor Frank."

"Now, now, you must not agitate yourself."

"But he has. First they pretend that he tried to murder this Mr. Blunt and not content with that they've accused him of murdering poor Mr. Morley."

Hercule Poirot coughed. He said, "I was down there, you know, at Exsham, when the shot was fired at Mr. Blunt."

Gladys Nevill said with a somewhat confusing use of

pronouns, "But even if Frank did—did do a foolish thing like that—and he's one of those Imperial Shirts, you know —they march with banners and have a ridiculous salute, and, of course, I suppose Mr. Blunt's wife *was* a very prominent Jewess, and they just work up these poor young men—quite harmless ones like Frank—until they think they are doing something wonderful and patriotic."

"Is that Mr. Carter's defense?" asked Hercule Poirot.

"Oh, *no*. Frank just swears he didn't do anything and had never seen the pistol before. I haven't spoken to him, of course—they wouldn't let me—but he's got a solicitor acting for him and he told me what Frank had said. Frank just says it's all a frame-up."

Poirot murmured, "And the solicitor is of the opinion that his client had better think of a more plausible story?"

"Lawyers are so difficult. They won't say anything *straight out*. But it's the murder charge I'm worrying about. Oh! M. Poirot, I'm sure Frank *couldn't* have killed Mr. Morley. I mean really—he hadn't any reason to."

"Is it true," said Poirot, "that when he came round that morning he had not yet got a job of any kind?"

"Well, really, M. Poirot, I don't see what difference *that* makes. Whether he got the job in the morning or the afternoon can't matter."

Poirot said, "But his story was that he came to tell you about his good luck. Now, it seems, he had as yet had no luck. Why, then, did he come?"

"Well, M. Poirot, the poor boy was dispirited and upset, and to tell the truth I believe he'd been drinking a little. Poor Frank has rather a weak head—and the drink upset him and so he felt like—like making a row, and he came round to Queen Charlotte Street to have it out with Mr. Morley, because, you see, Frank is awfully sensitive and it had upset him a lot to feel that Mr. Morley disapproved of him, and was what he called poisoning my mind."

"So he conceived the idea of making a scene in business

hours?"

"Well—yes—I suppose that *was* his idea. Of course, it was very wrong of Frank to think of such a thing."

Poirot looked thoughtfully at the tearful blond young woman in front of him.

He said, "Did you know that Frank Carter had a pistol—or a pair of pistols?"

"Oh, no, M. Poirot. I swear I didn't. And I don't believe it's true, either."

Poirot shook his head slowly in a perplexed manner.

"Oh! M. Poirot, do help us. If I could only feel that you were on our side—"

Poirot said, "I do not take sides. I am on the side only of the truth."

After he had got rid of the girl, Poirot rang up Scotland Yard. Japp had not yet returned but Detective Sergeant Beddoes was obliging and informative.

The police had not as yet found any evidence to prove Frank Carter's possession of the pistol before the assault at Exsham.

Poirot hung up the receiver thoughtfully. It was a point in Carter's favor. But so far it was the only one.

He had also learned from Beddoes a few more details as to the statement Frank Carter had made about his employment as gardener at Exsham. He stuck to his story of a secret service job. He had been given money in advance and some testimonials as to his gardening abilities and been told to apply to Mr. MacAlister, the head gardener, for the post. His instructions were to listen to the other gardeners' conversations and sound them as to their "red" tendencies, and to pretend to be a bit of a "red" himself. He had been interviewed and instructed in his task by a woman who had told him that she was known as Q.H.56 and that he had been recommended to her as a strong anti-communist. She had interviewed him in a dim light and he did not think he would know her again. She was a red-haired lady with a lot of make-up on.

Poirot groaned. The Phillips Oppenheim touch seemed to be reappearing.

He was tempted to consult Mr. Barnes on the subject. According to Mr. Barnes these things happened.

The last post brought him something which disturbed him more still.

A cheap envelope addressed in an unformed handwriting, postmarked Hertfordshire.

Poirot opened it and read:

Dear Sir,

Hoping as you will forgive me for troubling you, but I am very worried and do not know what to do. I do not want to be mixed up with the police in any way. I know that perhaps I ought to have told something I know before, but as they said the master had shot himself it was all right I thought. And I wouldn't have liked to get Miss Nevill's young man into trouble and never thought really for one moment as he had done it. But now I see he has been took up for shooting at a gentleman in the country and so perhaps he isn't quite all there and I ought to say but I thought I would write to you, you being a friend of the mistress and asking me so particular the other day if there was anything and of course I wish now I had told you then. But I do hope it won't mean getting mixed up with the police because I shouldn't like that and my mother wouldn't like it either. She has always been most particular.

Yours respectfully,

Agnes Fletcher.

Poirot murmured, "I always knew it was something to do with some man. I guessed the wrong man, that is all."

Chapter Eight

FIFTEEN, SIXTEEN, MAIDS IN THE KITCHEN

THE INTERVIEW WITH AGNES FLETCHER took place in Hertfordshire, in a somewhat derelict tea shop, for Agnes had been anxious not to tell her story under Miss Morley's critical eye.

The first quarter of an hour was taken up in listening to exactly how particular Agnes's mother had always been. Also, how Agnes's father, though a proprietor of licensed premises, had never once had any friction with the police, closing time being strictly observed to the second, and indeed Agnes's father and mother were universally respected and looked up to in Little Darlingham, Gloucestershire, and none of Mrs. Fletcher's family of six (two having died in infancy) had ever occasioned their parents the least anxiety. And if Agnes, now, were to get mixed up with the police in any way, Mum and Dad would probably die of it, because as she'd been saying, they'd always held their heads high, and never had no trouble of any kind with the police.

After this had been repeated, *da capo,* and with various embellishments, several times, Agnes drew a little nearer to the subject of the interview.

"I wouldn't like to say anything to Miss Morley, sir, because it might be, you see, that she'd say as how I ought to have said something before, but me and cook, we talked it over and we didn't see as it was any business of ours, because we'd read quite clear and plain in the paper as how the master had made a mistake in the drug he was giving and that he'd shot himself and the pistol was in his hands and everything, so it did seem quite clear, didn't it, sir?"

an OVERDOSE of DEATH   159

"When did you begin to feel differently?" Poirot hoped to get a little nearer the promised revelation by an encouraging but not too direct question.

Agnes replied promptly, "Seeing it in the paper about that Frank Carter—Miss Nevill's young man as was. When I read as he'd shot at that gentleman where he was gardener, well, I thought, it looks as if he *might* be queer in the head, because I do know there's people it takes like that, think they're being persecuted, or something, and that they're ringed round by enemies, and in the end it's dangerous to keep them at home and they have to be took away to the asylum. And I thought that maybe that Frank Carter was like that, because I did remember that he used to go on about Mr. Morley and say as Mr. Morley was against him and trying to separate him from Miss Nevill, but, of course, she wouldn't hear a word against him, and quite right, too, we thought—Emma and me, because you couldn't deny as Mr. Carter was very nice-looking and quite the gentleman. But, of course, neither of us thought he'd really done anything to Mr. Morley. We just thought it was a bit queer if you know what I mean."

Poirot said patiently, "What was queer?"

"It was that morning, sir, the morning Mr. Morley shot himself. I'd been wondering if I dared run down and get the post. The postman had come but that Alfred hadn't brought up the letters, which he wouldn't do, not unless there was some for Miss Morley or Mr. Morley, but if it was just for Emma or me he wouldn't bother to bring them up till lunchtime.

"So I went out on the landing and I looked down over the stairs. Miss Morley didn't like us going down to the hall, not during the master's business hours, but I thought maybe as I'd see Alfred taking in a patient to the master and I'd call down to him as he came back."

Agnes gasped, took a deep breath and went on.

"And it was then I saw him—that Frank Carter, I mean.

Halfway up the stairs he was—our stairs, I mean, above the master's floor. And he was standing there waiting and looking down—and I've come to feel more and more as though there was something *queer* about it. He seemed to be listening very intent, if you know what I mean."

"What time was this?"

"It must have been getting on for half past twelve, sir. And just as I was thinking, there, now, it's Frank Carter, and Miss Nevill's away for the day and *won't* he be disappointed, and I was wondering if I ought to run down and tell him because it looked as though that lump of an Alfred had forgot, otherwise I thought he wouldn't have been waiting for her. And just as I was hesitating, Mr. Carter, he seemed to make up his mind, and he slipped down the stairs very quick and went along the passage toward the master's surgery, and I thought to myself, the master won't like *that,* and I wondered if there was going to be a row. But just then Emma called me, said whatever was I up to? and I went up again and then, afterward, I heard the master had shot himself and, of course, it was so awful it just drove everything out of my head. But later, when that police inspector had gone I said to Emma, I said, I didn't say anything about Mr. Carter having been up with the master this morning, and she said was he? and I told her, and she said well, perhaps I *ought* to tell, but anyway I said I'd better wait a bit, and she agreed, because neither of us didn't want to get Frank Carter into trouble if we could help. And then, when it came to the inquest and it come out that the master had made that mistake in a drug and really had got panicky and shot himself, quite natural-like—well, then, of course, there was no call to say anything. But reading that piece in the paper two days ago—oh, it did give me a turn! And I said to myself, if he's one of those loonies that thinks they're persecuted and goes round shooting people, well, then maybe he *did* shoot the master after all!"

Her eyes, anxious and scared, looked hopefully at Hercule Poirot. He put as much reassurance into his voice as he could.

"You may be sure that you have done absolutely the right thing in telling me, Agnes," he said.

"Well, I must say, sir, it does take a load off my mind. You see, I've kept saying to myself as perhaps I *ought* to tell. And then, you see, I thought of getting mixed up with the police and what Mother would say. She's always been so particular about us all—"

"Yes, yes," said Hercule Poirot hastily.

He had had, he felt, as much of Agnes's mother as he could stand for one afternoon.

Poirot called at Scotland Yard and asked for Japp. When he was taken up to the Chief Inspector's room, "I want to see Carter," said Hercule Poirot.

Japp shot him a quick, sideways glance.

He said, "What's the big idea?"

"You are unwilling?"

Japp shrugged his shoulders. He said, "Oh, *I* shan't make objections. No good if I did. Who's the Home Secretary's little pet? You are. Who's got half the Cabinet in his pocket? You have. Hushing up their scandals for them."

Poirot's mind flew for a moment to that case that he had named the Case of the Augean Stables. He murmured, not without complacence, "It was ingenious, yes? You must admit it. Well imagined, let us say."

"Nobody but you would ever have thought of such a thing! Sometimes, Poirot, I think you haven't any scruples at all!"

Poirot's face became suddenly grave. He said, "That is not true."

"Oh, all right, Poirot, I didn't mean it. But you're so pleased sometimes with your damned ingenuity. What do you want to see Carter for? To ask him whether he really murdered Morley?"

To Japp's surprise, Poirot nodded his head emphatically.

"Yes, my friend, that is exactly the reason."

"And I suppose you think he'll tell you if he did?"

Japp laughed as he spoke. But Hercule Poirot remained grave. He said, "He might tell me—yes."

Japp looked at him curiously. He said, "You know, I've known you a long time—twenty years? Something like that. But I still don't always catch on to what you're driving at. I know you've got a bee in your bonnet about young Frank Carter. For some reason or other, you don't *want* him to be guilty—"

Hercule Poirot shook his head energetically.

"No, no, there you are wrong. It is the other way about—"

"I thought perhaps it was on account of that girl of his— the blond piece. You're a sentimental old buzzard in some ways—"

Poirot was immediately indignant.

"It is not I who am sentimental! That is an English failing! It is in England that they weep over young sweethearts and dying mothers and devoted children. Me, I am logical. If Frank Carter is a killer, then I am certainly not sentimental enough to wish to unite him in marriage to a nice but commonplace girl who, if he is hanged, will forget him in a year or two and find someone else."

"Then why don't you want to believe he is guilty?"

"I *do* want to believe he is guilty."

"I suppose you mean that you've got hold of something which more or less conclusively proves him to be innocent? Why hold it up, then? You ought to play fair with us, Poirot."

"I *am* playing fair with you. Presently, very shortly, I will give you the name and address of a witness who will be invaluable to you for the prosecution. Her evidence ought to clinch the case against him."

"But then— Oh! You've got me all tangled up. Why are you so anxious to see him?"

"To satisfy *myself,*" said Hercule Poirot.

And he would say no more.

Frank Carter, haggard, white-faced, still feebly inclined to bluster, looked on his unexpected visitor with unconcealed disfavor. He said rudely, "So it's you, you ruddy little foreigner? What do *you* want?"

"I want to see you and talk to you."

"Well, you see me all right. But I won't talk. Not without my lawyer. That's right, isn't it? You can't go against that. I've got the right to have my solicitor present before I say a word."

"Certainly you have. You can send for him if you like— but I should prefer that you did not."

"I daresay. Think you're going to trap me into making some damaging admissions, eh?"

"We are quite alone, remember."

"That's a bit unusual, isn't it? Got your police pals listening in, I've no doubt."

"You are wrong. This is a private interview between you and me."

Frank Carter laughed. He looked cunning and unpleasant. He said, "Come off it! You don't take me in with that old gag."

"Do you remember a girl called Agnes Fletcher?"

"Never heard of her."

"I think you will remember her, though you may never have taken much notice of her. She was house-parlormaid at fifty-eight Queen Charlotte Street."

"Well, what of it?"

Hercule Poirot said slowly, "On the morning of the day that Mr. Morley was shot, this girl Agnes happened to look over the banisters from the top floor. She saw you on the stairs—waiting and listening. Presently she saw you go along to Mr. Morley's room. The time was then twenty-six minutes or thereabouts past twelve."

Frank Carter trembled violently. Sweat came out on his brow. His eyes, more furtive than ever, went wildly from side to side. He shouted angrily, "It's a lie! It's a damned lie! You've paid her—the police have paid her—to say she saw me."

"At that time," said Hercule Poirot, "by your own account, you had left the house and were walking in the Marylebone Road."

"So I was. That girl's lying. She couldn't have seen me. It's a dirty plot. If it's true, why didn't she say so before?"

Hercule Poirot said quietly, "She did mention it at the time to her friend and colleague the cook. They were worried and puzzled and didn't know what to do. When a verdict of suicide was brought in they were much relieved and decided that it wasn't necessary for them to say anything."

"I don't believe a word of it! They're in it together, that's all. A couple of dirty, lying little—"

He tailed off into furious profanity.

Hercule Poirot waited.

When Carter's voice at last ceased, Poirot spoke again, still in the same calm, measured voice.

"Anger and foolish abuse will not help you. These girls are going to tell their story and it is going to be believed. Because, you see, they are telling the truth. The girl, Agnes Fletcher, *did* see you. You *were* there on the stairs at that time. You had *not* left the house. And you *did* go into Mr. Morley's room."

He paused and then asked quietly, "What happened then?"

"It's a lie, I tell you!"

Hercule Poirot felt very tired—very old. He did not like

Frank Carter. He disliked him very much. In his opinion
Frank Carter was a bully, a liar, a swindler—altogether
the type of young man the world could well do without.
He, Hercule Poirot, had only to stand back and let this
young man persist in his lies and the world would be rid
of one of its most unpleasant inhabitants.

Hercule Poirot said, "I suggest that you tell me the
truth—"

He realized the issue very clearly. Frank Carter was
stupid—but he wasn't so stupid as not to see that to persist
in his denial was his best and safest course. Let him once
admit that he *had* gone into that room at twenty-six minutes past twelve and he was taking a step into grave danger. For after that, any story he told would have a good
chance of being considered a lie.

Let him persist in his denial, then. If so, Hercule Poirot's
duty would be over. Frank Carter would in all probability
be hanged for the murder of Henry Morley—and it might
be, justly hanged.

Hercule Poirot had only to get up and go.

Frank Carter said again, "It's a lie!"

There was a pause. Hercule Poirot did not get up and
go. He would have liked to do so—very much. Nevertheless, he remained.

He leaned forward. He said—and his voice held all the
compelling force of his powerful personality—"I am not
lying to you. I ask you to believe me. If you did not kill
Morley your only hope is to tell me the *exact truth* of what
happened that morning."

The mean, treacherous face looking at him wavered,
became uncertain. Frank Carter pulled at his lip. His eyes
went from side to side, terrified, frankly animal eyes.

It was touch and go now.

Then suddenly, overborne by the strength of the personality confronting him, Frank Carter surrendered.

He said hoarsely, "All right, then—I'll tell you. God

curse you if you let me down now! I did go in. I went up
the stairs and waited till I could be sure of getting him
alone. Waited there, up above Morley's landing. Then a
gent came out and went down—fat gent. I was just making
up my mind to go—when another gent came out of Morley's room and went down, too. I knew I'd got to be quick.
I went along and nipped into his room without knocking.
I was all set to have it out with him. Mucking about,
putting my girl against me—damn him—"

He stopped.

"Yes?" said Hercule Poirot, and his voice was still urgent
—compelling—

Carter's voice croaked uncertainly.

"And he was lying there—dead. It's true! I swear it's
true! Lying just as they said at the inquest. I couldn't believe it at first. I stooped over him. But he was dead all
right. His hand was stone cold and I saw the bullet hole
in his head with a crust of blood round it—"

At the memory of it, sweat broke out on his forehead
again.

"I saw then I was in a jam. They'd go and say *I'd* done
it. I hadn't touched anything except his hand and the door
handle. I wiped that with my handkerchief, both sides, as
I went out, and I stole downstairs as quickly as I could.
There was nobody in the hall and I let myself out and
legged it away as fast as I could. No wonder I felt queer."

He paused. His scared eyes went to Poirot.

"That's the truth. *I swear that's the truth. He was dead
already.* You've got to believe me!"

Poirot got up. He said—and his voice was tired and sad—
"I believe you."

He moved toward the door.

Frank Carter cried out, "They'll hang me—they'll hang
me for sure if they know that I was in there."

Poirot said, "By telling the truth you have saved yourself
from being hanged."

"I don't see it. They'll say—"

Poirot interrupted him.

"Your story has confirmed what I knew to be the truth. You can leave it now to me."

He went out.

He was not at all happy.

He reached Mr. Barnes's house at Ealing at 6:45. He remembered that Mr. Barnes had called that a good time of day.

Mr. Barnes was at work in his garden.

He said by way of greeting, "We need rain, M. Poirot— need it badly."

He looked thoughtfully at his guest. He said, "You don't look very well, M. Poirot?"

"Sometimes," said Hercule Poirot, "I do not like the things I have to do."

Mr. Barnes nodded his head sympathetically.

He said, "I know."

Hercule Poirot looked vaguely round at the neat arrangement of the small beds. He murmured, "It is well-planned, this garden. Everything is to scale. It is small but exact."

Mr. Barnes said, "When you have only a small place you've got to make the most of it. You can't afford to make mistakes in the planning."

Hercule Poirot nodded.

Barnes went on, "I see you've got your man?"

"Frank Carter?"

"Yes. I'm rather surprised, really."

"You did not think that it was, so to speak, a private murder?"

"No. Frankly I didn't. What with Amberiotis and Alistair Blunt—I made sure that it was one of these espionage or counter-espionage mix-ups."

"That is the view you expounded to me at our first

meeting."

"I know. I was quite sure of it at the time."

Poirot said slowly, "But you were wrong."

"Yes. Don't rub it in. The trouble is, one goes by one's own experience. I've been mixed up in that sort of thing so much I suppose I'm inclined to see it everywhere."

Poirot said, "You have observed in your time a conjurer offer a card, have you not? What is called—forcing a card?"

"Yes, of course."

"That is what was done here. Every time that one thinks of a private reason for Morley's death, hey, presto!—the card is forced on one. Amberiotis, Alistair Blunt, the unsettled state of politics—of the country—" He shrugged his shoulders. "As for you, Mr. Barnes, you did more to mislead me than anybody."

"Oh, I say, Poirot, I'm sorry. I suppose that's true."

"You were in a position to *know*, you see. So your words carried weight."

"Well—I believed what I said. That's the only apology I can make."

He paused and sighed.

"And all the time, it was a purely private motive?"

"Exactly. It has taken me a long time to see the reason for the murder—although I had one very definite piece of luck."

"What was that?"

"A fragment of a conversation. Really, a very illuminating fragment if only I had had the sense to realize its significance at the time."

Mr. Barnes scratched his nose thoughtfully with the trowel. A small piece of earth adhered to the side of his nose.

"Being rather cryptic, aren't you?" he asked genially.

Hercule Poirot shrugged his shoulders. He said, "I am, perhaps, aggrieved that you were not more frank with me."

"I?"

"Yes."

"My dear fellow—I never had the least idea of Carter's guilt. As far as I knew, he'd left the house long before Morley was killed. I suppose now they've found he didn't leave when he said he did?"

Poirot said, "Carter was in the house at twenty-six minutes past twelve. He actually *saw* the murderer."

"Then Carter didn't—"

"Carter saw the murderer, I tell you!"

Mr. Barnes said, "Did—did he recognize him?"

Slowly Hercule Poirot shook his head.

Chapter Nine

SEVENTEEN, EIGHTEEN, MAIDS IN WAITING

ON THE FOLLOWING DAY Hercule Poirot spent some hours with a theatrical agent of his acquaintance. In the afternoon he went to Oxford. On the day after that he drove down to the country—it was late when he returned.

He had telephoned before he left to make an appointment with Mr. Alistair Blunt for that same evening.

It was half past nine when he reached the Gothic House.

Alistair Blunt was alone in his library when Poirot was shown in.

He looked an eager question at his visitor as he shook hands.

He said, "Well?"

Slowly Hercule Poirot nodded his head.

Blunt looked at him in almost incredulous appreciation.

"Have you found her?"

"Yes. Yes, I have found her."

He sat down. And he sighed.

Alistair Blunt said, "You are tired?"

"Yes. I am tired. And it is not pretty—what I have to tell you."

Blunt said, "Is she dead?"

"That depends," said Hercule Poirot slowly, "on how you like to look at it."

Blunt frowned.

He said, "My dear man, a person *must* be dead or alive. Miss Sainsbury Seale must be one or the other?"

"Ah, but who is Miss Sainsbury Seale?"

Alistair Blunt said, "You don't mean that—that there isn't any such person?"

"Oh, no, no. There was such a person. She lived in Calcutta. She taught elocution. She busied herself with good works. She came to England in the *Maharanah*—the same boat in which Mr. Amberiotis traveled. Although they were not in the same class, he helped her over something—some fuss about her luggage. He was, it would seem, a kindly man in little ways. And sometimes, Mr. Blunt, kindness is repaid in an unexpected fashion. It was so, you know, with Mr. Amberiotis. He chanced to meet the lady again in the streets of London. He was feeling expansive, he good-naturedly invited her to lunch with him at the Savoy. An unexpected treat for her. And an unexpected windfall for Mr. Amberiotis! For his kindness was not premeditated—he had no idea that this faded, middle-aged lady was going to present him with the equivalent of a gold mine. But, nevertheless, that is what she did, though she never suspected the fact herself.

"She was never, you see, of the first order of intelligence. A good, well-meaning soul, but the brain, I should say, of a hen."

Blunt said, "Then it wasn't she who killed the Chapman woman?"

Poirot said slowly, "It is difficult to know just how to present the matter. I shall begin, I think, where the matter began for me. With a *shoe!*"

Blunt said blankly, "With a *shoe?*"

Hercule Poirot nodded.

"Yes, a buckled shoe. I came out from my séance at the dentist's and as I stood on the steps of fifty-eight Queen Charlotte Street, a taxi stopped outside, the door opened, and a woman's foot prepared to descend. I am a man who notices a woman's foot and ankle. It was a well-shaped foot, with a good ankle and an expensive stocking, but I did not like the shoe. It was a new, shining, patent-leather shoe with a large ornate buckle. Not chic—not at all chic!

"And whilst I was observing this, the rest of the lady

came into sight—and frankly it was a disappointment—a middle-aged lady without charm and badly dressed."

"Miss Sainsbury Seale?"

"Precisely. As she descended a contretemps occurred—she caught the buckle of her shoe in the door and it was wrenched off. I picked it up and returned it to her. That was all. The incident was closed.

"Later, on that same day, I went with Chief Inspector Japp to interview the lady. She had not as yet sewed on the buckle, by the way.

"On that same evening, Miss Sainsbury Seale walked out of her hotel and vanished. That, we shall say, is Part One.

"Part Two began when Chief Inspector Japp summoned me to King Leopold Mansions. There was a fur chest in a flat there, and in that fur chest there had been found a body. I went into the room, I walked up to the chest—and the first thing I saw was a shabby buckled shoe!"

"Well?"

"You have not appreciated the point. It was a *shabby* shoe—a *well-worn* shoe. But you see, Miss Sainsbury Seale had come to King Leopold Mansions on the evening of that same day—the day of Mr. Morley's murder. In the morning the shoes were *new* shoes—in the evening they were *old* shoes. One does not wear out a pair of shoes in a day, you comprehend."

Alistair Blunt said without much interest, "She could have two pairs of shoes, I suppose?"

"Ah, *but that was not so.* For Japp and I had gone up to her room at the Glengowrie Court and had looked at all her possessions—and there was no pair of buckled shoes there. She might have had an old pair of shoes, yes. She might have changed into them after a tiring day to go out in the evening, yes? But if so, the other pair would have been at the hotel. It was curious, you will admit?"

Blunt smiled a little. He said, "I can't see that it is important."

"No, not important. Not at all important. But one does not like things that one cannot explain. I stood by the fur chest and I looked at the shoe—the buckle had recently been sewed on by hand. I will confess that I then had a moment of doubt—of myself. Yes, I said to myself, 'Hercule Poirot, you were a little light-headed perhaps this morning. You saw the world through rosy spectacles. Even the old shoes looked like new ones to you!' "

"Perhaps that *was* the explanation?"

"But, no, it was *not*. My eyes do not deceive me! To continue, I studied the dead body of this woman and I did not like what I saw. Why had the face been wantonly, deliberately smashed and rendered unrecognizable?"

Alistair Blunt moved restlessly. He said, "Must we go over that again? We know—"

Hercule Poirot said firmly, "It is necessary. I have to take you over the steps that led me at last to the truth. I said to myself, 'Something is wrong here. Here is a dead woman in the clothes of Miss Sainsbury Seale—except, perhaps, the shoes?—and with the handbag of Miss Sainsbury Seale—but why is her face unrecognizable? Is it, perhaps, because the face is not the face of Miss Sainsbury Seale?' And immediately I begin to put together what I have heard of the appearance of the *other* woman—the woman to whom the flat belongs, and I ask myself—might it not, perhaps be *this other woman* who lies dead here? I go then and look at the other woman's bedroom. I try to picture to myself what sort of woman she is. In superficial appearance, very different to the other. Smart, showily dressed, very much made up. But in essentials, *not unlike*. Hair, build, age— But there is one difference. Mrs. Albert Chapman took a five in shoes. Miss Sainsbury Seale, I knew, took a size nine stocking—that is to say she would take at least a six in shoes. Mrs. Chapman, then, had smaller feet than Miss Sainsbury Seale. I went back to the body. If my half-formed idea were right, and the body was that of Mrs. Chapman wearing Miss Sainsbury Seale's clothes, *then the shoes should be too big.* I took hold of one. But it was not loose. It fitted tightly. That looked as though it *were* the body of Miss Sainsbury Seale after all! But in that case, *why* was the face disfigured? Her identity was already proved by the handbag, which could easily have been removed, but which had *not* been removed.

"It was a puzzle—a tangle. In desperation I seized on Mrs. Chapman's address book—a dentist was the only person who could prove definitely who the dead woman was—or was not. By a coincidence, Mrs. Chapman's dentist was Mr. Morley. Morley was dead, but identification was still possible. You know the result. The body was identified in the coroner's court by Mr. Morley's successor as that of Mrs. Albert Chapman."

Blunt was fidgeting with some impatience, but Poirot took no notice. He went on.

"I was left now with a psychological problem. What sort of a woman was Mabelle Sainsbury Seale? There were two answers to that question. The first was the obvious one borne out by her whole life in India and by the testimony of her personal friends. That depicted her as an earnest, conscientious, slightly stupid woman. Was there another Miss Sainsbury Seale? Apparently there was. There was a woman who had lunched with a well-known foreign agent, who had accosted you in the street and claimed to be a close friend of your wife's—a statement that was almost certainly untrue—a woman who had left a man's house very shortly before a murder had been committed, a woman who had visited another woman on the evening when in all probability that other woman had been murdered, and who had since disappeared, although she must be aware that the police force of England was looking for her. Were all these actions compatible with the character which her friends gave her? It would seem that they were not. Therefore, if Miss Sainsbury Seale were *not* the good, amiable creature she seemed, then it would appear that she was quite possibly a cold-blooded murderess, or almost certainly an accomplice after the fact.

"I had one more criterion—my own personal impression. I had talked to Mabelle Sainsbury Seale myself. How had she struck *me?* And that, Mr. Blunt, was the most difficult question to answer of all. Everything that she said, her way of talking, her manner, her gestures, all were perfectly in accord with her given character. *But they were equally in accord with a clever actress playing a part.* And, after all, Mabelle Sainsbury Seale had started life as an actress.

"I had been much impressed by a conversation I had had with Mr. Barnes of Ealing who had also been a patient at fifty-eight Queen Charlotte Street on that particular day. His theory, expressed very forcibly, was that the deaths of Morley and of Amberiotis were only incidental, so to speak—that the intended victim was *you.*"

Alistair Blunt said, "Oh, come now—that's a bit far-fetched."

"Is it, Mr. Blunt? Is it not true that at this moment there are various groups of people to whom it is vital that you should be—removed, shall we say? Shall be no longer capable of exerting your influence?"

Blunt said, "Oh, yes, that's true enough. But why mix up this business of Morley's death with that?"

Poirot said, "Because there is a certain—how shall I put it?—lavishness about the case—expense is no object—human life is no object. Yes, there is a recklessness, a lavishness—that points to a *big* crime!"

"You don't think Morley shot himself because of a mistake?"

"I never thought so—not for a minute. No, Morley was

murdered, Amberiotis was murdered, an unrecognizable woman was murdered— *Why?* For some big stake. Barnes's theory was that somebody had tried to bribe Morley or his partner to put you out of the way."

Alistair Blunt said sharply, "Nonsense!"

"Ah, but is it nonsense? Say one wishes to put someone out of the way. Yes, but that someone is forewarned, forearmed, difficult of access. To kill that person it is necessary to be able to approach him without awakening his suspicions—and where would a man be less suspicious than in a dentist's chair?"

"Well, that's true, I suppose. I never thought of it like that."

"It *is* true. And once I realized it I had my first vague glimmering of the truth."

"So you accepted Barnes's theory? Who is Barnes, by the way?"

"Barnes was Reilly's twelve o'clock patient. He is retired from the Home Office and lives at Ealing. An insignificant little man. But you are wrong when you say I accepted his theory. I did not. I only accepted the *principle* of it."

"What do you mean?"

Hercule Poirot said, "All along, all the way through, I have been led astray—sometimes unwittingly, sometimes deliberately and for a purpose. All along it was presented to me, *forced* upon me, that this was what you might call a *public* crime. That is to say, that you, Mr. Blunt, were the focus of it all, in your *public* character. You, the banker, you, the controller of finance, you, the upholder of conservative tradition!

"But every public character has a *private* life also. That was my mistake, *I forgot the private life*. There existed *private* reasons for killing Morley—Frank Carter's, for instance.

"There could also exist private reasons for killing *you*—

You had relations who would inherit money when you died. You had people who loved and hated you—as a *man* —not as a public figure.

"And so I came to the supreme instance of what I call 'the forced card.' The purported attack upon you by Frank Carter. If that attack was genuine—then it *was* a political crime. But was there any other explanation? *There could be.* There was a second man in the shrubbery. The man who rushed up and seized Carter. A man who could easily have fired that shot and then tossed the pistol to Carter's feet so that the latter would almost inevitably pick it up and be found with it in his hand.

"I considered the problem of Howard Raikes. Raikes had been at Queen Charlotte Street that morning of Morley's death. Raikes was a bitter enemy of all that you stood for and were. Yes, but Raikes was something more. *Raikes was the man who might marry your niece,* and with you dead, your niece would inherit a very handsome income, even though you had prudently arranged that she could not touch the principal.

"Was the whole thing, after all, a *private* crime—a crime for *private* gain, for *private* satisfaction? Why had I thought it a *public* crime? *Because, not once, but many times, that idea had been suggested to me, had been forced upon me like a forced card—*

"It was then, when that idea occurred to me, that I had my first glimmering of the truth. I was in church at the time and singing a verse of a psalm. It spoke of a snare laid with cords.

"A snare? Laid for me? Yes, it could be— But in that case *who* had laid it? *There was only one person who could have laid it.* And that did not make sense—or *did* it? Had I been looking at the case *upside down?* Money no object? Exactly! Reckless disregard of human life? Yes, again. For the stakes for which the guilty person was playing were *enormous.*

"But if this new, strange idea of mine was right, it must explain *everything*. It must explain, for instance, the mystery of the dual nature of Miss Sainsbury Seale. It must solve the riddle of the buckled shoe. And it must answer the question: *Where is Miss Sainsbury Seale now?*

"*Eh bien*—it did all that and more. It showed me that Miss Sainsbury Seale was the beginning and middle and end of the case. No wonder it had seemed to me that there were two Mabelle Sainsbury Seales. There *were* two Mabelle Sainsbury Seales. There was the good, stupid, amiable woman who was vouched for so confidently by her friends. And there was the other—the woman who was mixed up with two murders and who told lies and who vanished mysteriously.

"Remember, the porter at King Leopold Mansions said that Miss Sainsbury Seale had been there once before.

"In my reconstruction of the case, that first time was the only time. She never left King Leopold Mansions. *The other Miss Sainsbury Seale took her place.* That other Mabelle Sainsbury Seale, dressed in clothes of the same type and wearing a new pair of shoes with buckles because the others were too large for her, went to the Russell Square Hotel at a busy time of day, packed up the dead woman's clothes, paid the bill, and left. She went to the Glengowrie Court Hotel. None of the real Miss Sainsbury Seale's friends saw her after that time, remember. She played the part of Mabelle Sainsbury Seale there for over a week. She wore Mabelle Sainsbury Seale's clothes, she talked in Mabelle Sainsbury Seale's voice, but she had to buy a smaller pair of evening shoes, too. And then—she vanished, her last appearance being when she was seen reentering King Leopold Mansions on the evening of the day Morley was killed."

"Are you trying to say," demanded Alistair Blunt, "that it *was* Mabelle Sainsbury Seale's dead body in that flat, after all?"

"Of course it was! It was a very clever double bluff—the smashed face was *meant* to raise a question of the woman's identity!"

"But the dental evidence?"

"Ah! Now we come to it. It was not the *dentist himself* who gave evidence. Morley was dead. He couldn't give evidence as to his own work. *He* would have known who the dead woman was. It was the *charts* that were put in as evidence—and the charts were faked. Both women were his patients, remember. All that had to be done was to relabel the charts, exchanging the names."

Hercule Poirot added, "And now you see what I meant when you asked me if the woman was dead and I replied, 'That depends.' For when you say, 'Miss Sainsbury Seale'—*which woman do you mean?* The woman who disappeared from the Glengowrie Court Hotel or the real Mabelle Sainsbury Seale?"

Alistair Blunt said, "I know, M. Poirot, that you have a great reputation. Therefore, I accept that you must have some grounds for this extraordinary assumption—for it is an assumption, nothing more. But all I can see is the fantastic improbability of the whole thing. You are saying, are you not, that Mabelle Sainsbury Seale was deliberately murdered and that Morley was also murdered to prevent his identifying her dead body. But *why?* That's what I want to know. Here's this woman—a perfectly harmless, middle-aged woman—with plenty of friends and apparently no enemies. Why on earth all this elaborate plot to get rid of her?"

"Why? Yes, that is the question. *Why?* As you say, Mabelle Sainsbury Seale was a perfectly harmless creature who wouldn't hurt a fly! Why, then, was she deliberately and brutally murdered? Well, I will tell you what I think."

"Yes?"

Hercule Poirot leaned forward. He said, "It is my belief that Mabelle Sainsbury Seale was murdered because she happened to have too good a memory for faces."

"What do you mean?"

Hercule Poirot said, "We have separated the dual personality. There is the harmless lady from India, and there is the clever actress playing the part of the harmless lady from India. But there is one incident that falls between the two roles. Which Miss Sainsbury Seale was it who spoke to you on the doorstep of Mr. Morley's house? She claimed, you will remember, to be 'a great friend of your wife's.' Now that claim was adjudged by her friends and by the light of ordinary probability to be untrue. So we can say, 'That was a lie. The real Miss Sainsbury Seale does not tell lies.' So it was a lie uttered by the impostor for a purpose of her own."

Alistair Blunt nodded.

"Yes, that reasoning is quite clear. Though I still don't know what the purpose was."

Poirot said, "Ah, *pardon*—but let us first look at it *the other way round*. It was the *real* Miss Sainsbury Seale. She does *not* tell lies. *So the story must be true.*"

"I suppose you *can* look at it that way—but it seems very unlikely—"

"Of course it is unlikely! But taking that second hypothesis as fact—the story is *true*. Therefore Miss Sainsbury Seale *did* know your wife. She knew her *well*. Therefore—*your wife must have been the type of person Miss Sainsbury Seale would have known well*. Someone in her own station of life. An Anglo-Indian—a missionary—or, to go back farther still—an actress— Therefore—*not* Rebecca Arnholt!

"Now, M. Blunt, do you see what I meant when I talked of a private and a public life? You are the great banker. But you are also a man who married a rich wife. And before you married her you were only a junior partner in the firm—not very long down from Oxford.

"You comprehend—I began to look at the case the *right*

way up. Expense no object? Naturally not—to you. Reckless of human life—that, too, since for a long time you have been virtually a dictator and to a dictator his own life becomes unduly important and those of others unimportant."

Alistair Blunt said, "What are you suggesting, M. Poirot?"

Poirot said quietly, "I am suggesting, Mr. Blunt, that when you married Rebecca Arnholt, *you were married already.* That, dazzled by the vista, not so much of wealth, as of power, you suppressed that fact and deliberately committed bigamy. That your real wife acquiesced in the situation."

"And who was this real wife?"

"Mrs. Albert Chapman was the name she went under at King Leopold Mansions—a handy spot, not five minutes' walk from your house on the Chelsea Embankment. You borrowed the name of a real secret agent, realizing that it would give support to her hints of a husband engaged in intelligence work. Your scheme succeeded perfectly. No suspicion was ever aroused. Nevertheless, the fact remained, *you had never been legally married to Rebecca Arnholt* and you were guilty of bigamy. You never dreamed of danger after so many years. It came out of the blue—in the form of a tiresome woman who remembered you after nearly twenty years, as her friend's husband. Chance brought her back to this country, chance let her meet you in Queen Charlotte Street—it was chance that your niece was with you and heard what she said to you. Otherwise I might never have guessed."

"I told you about that myself, my dear Poirot."

"No, it was your niece who insisted on telling me and you could not very well protest too violently in case it might arouse suspicions. And after that meeting, one more evil chance—from your point of view—occurred. Mabelle Sainsbury Seale met Amberiotis, went to lunch with him, and babbled to him of this meeting with a friend's husband—'after all these years! Looks older, of course, but had hardly changed!' That, I admit, is pure guesswork on my part but I believe it is what happened. I do not think that Mabelle Sainsbury Seale realized for a moment that the Mr. Blunt her friend had married was the shadowy figure behind the finance of the world. The name, after all, is not an uncommon one. But Amberiotis, remember, in addition to his espionage activities, was a blackmailer. Blackmailers have an uncanny nose for a secret. Amberiotis wondered. Easy to find out just who the Mr. Blunt was. And then, I have no doubt, he wrote to you—or telephoned. Oh, yes—a gold mine for Amberiotis."

Poirot paused, then went on.

"There is only one effectual method of dealing with a really efficient and experienced blackmailer. Silence him.

"It was not a case, as I had had erroneously suggested to me, of 'Blunt must go.' It was, on the contrary, 'Amberiotis must go.' But the answer was the same! The easiest way to get at a man is when he is off his guard, and when is a man more off his guard than in the dentist's chair?"

Poirot paused again. A faint smile came to his lips. He said, "The truth about the case was mentioned very early. The page boy, Alfred, was reading a crime story called *Death at 11:45*. We should have taken that as an omen. For, of course, that is just about the time when Morley was killed. You shot him just as you were leaving. Then you pressed his buzzer, turned on the taps of the wash basin, and left the room. You timed it so that you came down the stairs just as Alfred was taking the false Mabelle Sainsbury Seale to the elevator. You actually opened the front door, perhaps you passed out, but as the elevator doors shut and the elevator went up you slipped inside again and went up the stairs.

"I know, from my own visits, just what Alfred did when he took up a patient. He knocked on the door, opened it, and stood back to let the patient pass in. Inside the water was running—inference, Morley was washing his hands as usual. But Alfred couldn't actually *see* him.

"As soon as Alfred had gone down again in the elevator, you slipped along into the surgery. Together you and your accomplice lifted the body and carried it into the adjoining office. Then a quick hunt through the files, and the charts of Mrs. Chapman and Miss Sainsbury Seale were cleverly falsified. You put on a white linen coat, perhaps your wife applied a trace of make-up. But nothing much was needed. It was Amberiotis's first visit to Morley. He had never met you. And your photograph seldom appears in the papers. Besides, why should he have suspicions? A blackmailer does not fear his dentist. Miss Sainsbury Seale goes down and Alfred shows her out. The buzzer goes and Amberiotis is taken up. He finds the dentist washing his hands behind the door in approved fashion. He is conducted to the chair. He indicates the painful tooth. You talk the accustomed patter. You explain it will be best to freeze the gum. The procaine and adrenaline are there. You inject a big enough dose to kill. And incidentally he will not feel any lack of skill in your dentistry!

"Completely unsuspicious, Amberiotis leaves. You bring out Morley's body and arrange it on the floor, dragging it slightly on the carpet now that you have to manage it singlehanded. You wipe the pistol and put it in his hand—wipe the door handle so that your prints shall not be the last. The instruments you used have all been passed into the sterilizer. You leave the room, go down the stairs, and slip out of the front door at a suitable moment. That is your only moment of danger.

"It should all have passed off so well! Two people who threatened your safety—both dead. A third person also dead—but that, from your point of view, was unavoidable.

And all so easily explained. Morley's suicide explained by the mistake he had made over Amberiotis. The two deaths cancel out. One of these regrettable accidents.

"But alas for you, *I* am on the scene. *I* have doubts. *I* make objections. All is not going as easily as you hoped. So there must be a second line of defenses. There must be, if necessary, a scapegoat. You have already informed yourself minutely of Morley's household: There is this man, Frank Carter; he will do. So your accomplice arranges that he shall be engaged in a mysterious fashion as gardener. If, later, he tells such a ridiculous story no one will believe it. In due course, the body in the fur chest will come to light. At first it will be thought to be that of Miss Sainsbury Seale, then the dental evidence will be taken. Big sensation! It may seem a needless complication, but it was *necessary*. You do not want the police force of England to be looking for a missing Mrs. Albert Chapman. No, let Mrs. Chapman be dead—and let it be Mabelle Sainsbury Seale for whom the police look—since they can never find her. Besides, through your influence, you can arrange to have the case dropped.

"You did do that, but since it was necessary that you should know just what *I* was doing, you sent for me and urged me to find the missing woman for you. And you continued, steadily, to 'force a card' upon me. Your accomplice rang me up with a melodramatic warning—the same idea—espionage—the *public* aspect. She is a clever actress, this wife of yours, but to disguise one's voice the natural tendency is to imitate another voice. Your wife imitated the intonation of Mrs. Olivera. That puzzled me, I may say, a good deal.

"Then I was taken down to Exsham—the final performance was staged. How easy to arrange a loaded pistol amongst laurels so that a man, clipping them, shall unwittingly cause it to go off. The pistol falls at his feet. Startled, he picks it up. What more do you want? He is caught red-handed—with a ridiculous story and with a pistol which is a twin to the one with which Morley was shot.

"And all a snare for the feet of Hercule Poirot."

Alistair Blunt stirred a little in his chair. His face was grave and a little sad. He said, "Don't misunderstand me, M. Poirot. How much do you guess? And how much do you actually *know?*"

Poirot said, "I have a certificate of the marriage—at a registry office near Oxford—of Martin Alistair Blunt and Gerda Grant. Frank Carter saw two men leave Morley's surgery just after twenty-five past twelve. The first was a fat man—Amberiotis. The second was, of course, you. Frank Carter did not recognize you. He only saw you from above."

"How fair of you to mention that!"

"He went into the surgery and found Morley's body. The hands were cold and there was dried blood round the wound. That meant that Morley had been dead some time. Therefore the dentist who attended to Amberiotis could not have been Morley and must have been Morley's murderer."

"Anything else?"

"Yes. Helen Montressor was arrested this afternoon."

Alistair Blunt gave one sharp movement. Then he sat very still. He said, "That—rather tears it."

Hercule Poirot said, "Yes. The real Helen Montressor, your distant cousin, died in Canada seven years ago. You suppressed that fact, and took advantage of it."

A smile came to Alistair Blunt's lips. He spoke naturally and with a kind of boyish enjoyment.

"Gerda got a kick out of it all, you know. I'd like to make you understand. You're such a clever fellow. I married her without letting my people know. She was acting in repertory at the time. My people were the strait-laced kind, and I was going into the firm. We agreed to keep it dark. She went on acting. Mabelle Sainsbury Seale was in the company, too. She knew about us. Then she went abroad with a touring company. Gerda heard of her once or twice from India. Then she stopped writing. Mabelle got mixed up with some Hindu. She was always a stupid, credulous girl.

"I wish I could make you understand about my meeting with Rebecca and my marriage. Gerda understood. The only way I can put it is that it was like royalty. I had the chance of marrying a queen and playing the part of prince consort or even king. I looked on my marriage to Gerda as morganatic. I loved her. I didn't want to get rid of her. And the whole thing worked splendidly. I liked Rebecca immensely. She was a woman with a first-class financial brain and mine was just as good. We were good at team-work. It was supremely exciting. She was an excellent companion and I think I made her happy. I was genuinely sorry when she died. The queer thing was that Gerda and I grew to enjoy the secret thrill of our meetings. We had all sorts of ingenious devices. She was an actress by nature. She had a repertoire of seven or eight characters—Mrs. Albert Chapman was only one of them. She was an American widow in Paris. I met her there when I went over on business. And she used to go to Norway with painting things as an artist. I went there for the fishing. And then, later, I passed her off as my cousin, Helen Montressor. It was great fun for us both, and it kept romance alive, I suppose. We could have married officially after Rebecca died—but we didn't want to. Gerda would have found it hard to live my official life and, of course, something from the past *might* have been raked up, but I think the real reason we went on more or less the same was that we *enjoyed* the secrecy of it. We should have found open domesticity dull."

Blunt paused. He said, and his voice changed and hardened, "And then that damned fool of a woman messed up everything. Recognizing me—after all those years! And she told Amberiotis. You see—you *must* see—that something had to be done! It wasn't only myself—not only the selfish point of view. If I was ruined and disgraced—the country, *my* country was hit as well. For I've done something for England, M. Poirot. I've held it firm and kept it solvent. It's free from dictators—from Fascism and from Communism. I don't really care for money as money. I do like power—I like to rule—but I don't want to tyrannize. We *are* democratic in England—truly democratic. We can grumble and say what we think and laugh at our politicians. We're *free*. I care for all that—it's been my life work. But if *I* went—well, you know what would probably happen. I'm *needed*, M. Poirot. And a damned, double-crossing, blackmailing rogue of a Greek was going to destroy my life work. Something *had* to be done. Gerda saw it, too. We were sorry about the Sainsbury Seale woman—but it was no good. We'd got to silence her. She couldn't be trusted to hold her tongue. Gerda went to see her, asked her to tea, told her to ask for Mrs. Chapman, said she was staying in Mrs. Chapman's flat. Mabelle Sainsbury Seale came, quite unsuspecting. She never knew anything—the medinal was in the tea—it's quite painless. You just sleep and don't wake up. The face business was done afterward—rather sickening, but we felt it was necessary. Mrs. Chapman was to exit for good. I had given my 'cousin' Helen a cottage to live in. We decided that after a while we would get married. But first we had to get Amberiotis out of the way. It worked beautifully. He hadn't a suspicion that I wasn't a real dentist. I did my stuff with the hand-picks rather well. I didn't risk the drill. Of course, after the injection he couldn't feel what I was doing. Probably just as well!"

Poirot asked, "The pistols?"

"Actually they belonged to a secretary I once had in America. He bought them abroad somewhere. When he left he forgot to take them."

There was a pause. Then Alistair Blunt asked, "Is there anything else you want to know?"

Hercule Poirot said, "What about Morley?"

Alistair Blunt said simply, "I was sorry about Morley."

Hercule Poirot said, "Yes, I see—"

There was a long pause, then Blunt said, "Well, M. Poirot, what about it?"

Poirot said, "Helen Montressor is arrested already."

"And now it's my turn?"

"That was my meaning, yes."

Blunt said gently, "But you are not happy about it, eh?"

"No, I am not at all happy."

Alistair Blunt said, "I've killed three people. So presumably I *ought* to be hanged. But you've heard my defensc."

"Which is—exactly?"

"That I believe, with all my heart and soul, that I am necessary to the continued peace and well-being of this country."

Hercule Poirot allowed, "That may be—yes."

"You agree, don't you?"

"I agree, yes. You stand for all the things that to my mind are important. For sanity and balance and stability and honest dealing."

Alistair Blunt said quietly, "Thanks."

He added, "Well, what about it?"

"You suggest that I—retire from the case?"

"Yes."

"And your wife?"

"I've got a good deal of pull. Mistaken identity, that's the line to take."

"And if I refuse?"

"Then," said Alistair Blunt simply, "I'm for it."

He went on, "It's in your hands, Poirot. It's up to you. But I tell you this—and it's not just self-preservation—I'm needed in the world. And do you know why? Because I'm an honest man. And because I've got common sense—and no particular ax of my own to grind."

Poirot nodded. Strangely enough, he believed all that.

He said, "Yes, that is one side. You are the right man in the right place. You have sanity, judgment, balance. But there is the other side. Three human beings who are dead."

"Yes, but think of them! Mabelle Sainsbury Seale—you said yourself—a woman with the brains of a hen! Amberiotis—a crook and a blackmailer!"

"And Morley?"

"I've told you before. I'm sorry about Morley. But after all—he was a decent fellow and a good dentist—but there *are* other dentists."

"Yes," said Poirot, "there are other dentists. And Frank Carter? You would have let him die, too, without regret?"

Blunt said, "I don't waste any pity on *him*. He's no good. An utter rotter."

Poirot said, "But a human being—"

"Oh, well, we're all human beings."

"Yes, we are all human beings. That is what you have not remembered. You have said that Mabelle Sainsbury Seale was a foolish human being and Amberiotis an evil one, and Frank Carter a wastrel—and Morley—Morley was only a dentist and there are other dentists. That is where you and I, Mr. Blunt, do not see alike. For to me the lives of those four people were just as important as your life."

"You're wrong."

"No, I am not wrong. You are a man of great natural honesty and rectitude. You took one step aside—and outwardly it has not affected you. Publicly you have continued the same—upright, trustworthy, honest. But within you the love of power grew to overwhelming heights. So you sacrificed four human lives and thought them of no account."

"Don't you realize, Poirot, that the safety and happiness of the whole nation depend on me?"

"I am not concerned with nations, monsieur. I am concerned with the lives of private individuals who have the right not to have their lives taken from them."

He got up.

"So that's your answer," said Alistair Blunt.

Hercule Poirot said in a tired voice, "Yes—that is my answer."

He went to the door and opened it. Two men came in.

Hercule Poirot went down to where a girl was waiting.

Jane Olivera, her face white and strained, stood against the mantelpiece. Beside her was Howard Raikes.

She said, "Well?"

Poirot said gently, "It is all over."

Raikes said harshly, "What do you mean?"

Poirot said, "Mr. Alistair Blunt has been arrested for murder."

Raikes said, "I thought he'd buy you off."

Jane said, "No. *I* never thought that."

Poirot sighed. He said, "The world is yours. The new heaven and the new earth. In your new world, my children, let there be freedom and let there be pity. That is all I ask."

Chapter Ten

NINETEEN, TWENTY, MY PLATE'S EMPTY

HERCULE POIROT WALKED HOME along the deserted streets.

An unobtrusive figure joined him.

"Well?" said Mr. Barnes.

Hercule Poirot shrugged his shoulders and spread out his hands.

Barnes said, "What line did he take?"

"He admitted everything and pleaded justification. He said that this country needs him."

"So it does," said Mr. Barnes.

He added after a minute or two, "Don't you think so?"

"Yes, I do."

"Well, then—"

"We may be wrong," said Hercule Poirot.

"I never thought of that," said Mr. Barnes. "So we may."

They walked on for a little way, then Barnes asked curiously, "What are you thinking about?"

Hercule Poirot quoted: " 'Because thou hast rejected the word of the Lord, he hath also rejected thee from being king.' "

"Hm—I see—" said Mr. Barnes. "Saul—after the Amalekites. Yes, you could think of it that way."

They walked on a little farther, then Barnes said, "I take the tube here. Good night, Poirot." He paused, then said awkwardly, "You know—there's something I'd like to tell you."

"Yes, *mon ami?*"

"Feel I owe it to you. Led you astray unintentionally. Fact of the matter is, Albert Chapman, Q.X.912."

"Yes?"

"I'm Albert Chapman. That's partly why I was so interested. I knew, you see, that I'd never had a wife."

He hurried away, chuckling.

Poirot stood stock-still. Then his eyes opened, his eyebrows rose.

He said to himself, *"Nineteen, twenty, my plate's empty—"*

And went home.